THE BLOODY LIST
LETTERS FROM A SERIAL KILLER

DAVID MUSSER

Copyright © 2023 by David Musser

Layout design and Copyright © 2024 by Next Chapter

Published 2024 by Next Chapter

Edited by Tom Vater

Cover art by Jaylord Bonnit

Large Print Edition

This book is a work of fiction. Names, characters, places, and incidents are the product of the author's imagination or are used fictitiously. Any resemblance to actual events, locales, or persons, living or dead, is purely coincidental.

All rights reserved. No part of this book may be reproduced or transmitted in any form or by any means, electronic or mechanical, including photocopying, recording, or by any information storage and retrieval system, without the author's permission.

CONTENT WARNING

This book is a work of fiction, and it deals with mental illness, serial killing, rape, and many other issues that may be 'triggers,' not only in today's society but in society all along.

I'm David Musser. Most would say that I'm a nice guy, that quiet neighbor, and not the kind of guy who writes stories like this one. I write stories as they come to me, and wherever this story came from, it cost me a lot, both emotionally and mentally. I stopped and started writing it several times, and, in the end, I did my best to bring it to you as it came to me.

The main character is also a nice guy, and I do like his devotion to family; while we may have grown up in a similar and more leisurely time, a

CONTENT WARNING

time before social media and instant gratification, that is the extent of our similarities.

I put this here because if you're a friend of mine, someone I work with, or someone who cares about me, you may want to stop reading if you think it will impact your feelings for me.

This is fiction, so for those who dare, please read on, and I bet you will like Charlie before you've finished the book. I know I did at first. To say that this book came to me like an emotional roller coaster and that the ride was amazing would be an understatement.

P.S. Thank you for continuing to support my writing. I promise to be back with something nice and clean, maybe a zombie book or something where a monster destroys the earth. I believe that would be more socially acceptable.

This book is dedicated to all fans of Jeff Lindsay and other authors who have written about serial killers. Like you, I am a fan, and I hope that I do fictional justice to this horrific genre. Darkly Dreaming Dexter by Jeff Lindsay is one of my favorite in the genre.

In The Bloody List, I will take you into the mind of a serial killer, one that, while he has a pleasant name, is terrifying in his own right.

ACKNOWLEDGMENTS

Megan Anderson - You have been an invaluable part of my journey as my editor for the Keep in the Light series. Your belief in me and my work gave me the courage to start this adventure, and I am forever grateful for your support. I know that some of the scenes in my books kept you up at night, and for that, I apologize.

Rachel Musser - As my daughter, you are a constant source of love and support. I am so proud of the amazing person you have become, and I am grateful for everything you do. Your love helps me to get through each day, and I could not do what I do without you. Thank you for being such an incredible daughter and for always believing in me. I love you more than words can say.

Kim Huffman - your feedback on my writing has been invaluable. When I first started this journey, I never could have imagined the outpouring of support and encouragement from friends like yourself. Your insightful questions and comments have helped me grow as a writer, and I'm so grateful for your support.

Lisa Musser - As my wife and partner of over thirty years, you've been by my side through thick and thin. Life is never easy, but sticking together the way we have has enabled me to become the man I am.

Natalie Russell - As a relatively new author, I find it an amazing treat when someone is not only a fan but also cares enough to provide me with wonderful feedback and so many insights into my story.

CONTENTS

1. Pen Pals — 1
2. A Life so Normal — 25
3. Playing House — 40
4. Saying Goodbye — 52
5. Liam's Fall From Grace — 65
6. Preparing for War — 82
7. Five Hundred Ways to Die on a Sunday — 91
8. Vacation Day — 104
9. Stalking the Reporter — 113
10. Not Everyone is Perfect — 132
11. Governor Pratt — 139
12. Missing — 155
13. A Partner's Love — 160
14. Firefight — 165
15. Death of a Mother — 175
16. Hallowed Ground — 188
    Epilogue — 199

From The Author — 204
Music Playlist — 206
Newspaper Clippings — 208

1

PEN PALS

MILNER DAILY

THE ADONIS KILLER STRIKES AGAIN | FRIDAY APRIL 9, 2010 | PRICE $1.25

Police Receive Email from alleged serial killer 'Adonis'

The alleged perpetrator sent Detective Martinez the text of the old fable about the scorpion and the frog to explain his motivation. The contents of the email have not been released to the press. Detective Martinez has not commented on why she, rather than the investigating officer, received the email. When asked about the alleged serial killer's motivation, she said, "No comment."

Sketch of artist's rendering of Adonis released. The public is asked to keep vigilant.

FRIDAY, APRIL 9, 2010

Detective, you can call me Charlie. I wonder whether you ever had an imaginary friend? One that talked to you and played with you when you didn't have anyone else? Did you have someone like that -

the most amazing friend you ever had? Well, I did. His name was Whiro, but I just called him Whir.

Besides being my best friend, he was my only friend. The things he showed me were unique and wonderful. That is, until they weren't... I will tell you more about that later.

When I was young, he was the best friend anyone could ever have had. I remember lying on my bed, listening to his beautiful tales. I never watched much television. I was before the generation of children whose parents felt guilty for what they didn't have, and they overcompensated with multiple televisions in the home. I'm sure that is one cause for the family unit breaking up nowadays. Kids can be like - If I don't like what is playing on the television in the living room, I can go to my own room and watch whatever I want.

Some of the stories he told me involved things I would only come to understand later, but one tale I remember that set the stage for my life was about a scorpion and a frog. I'm sure you've heard it. Here goes if not.

A scorpion wants to cross a river but cannot swim, so it asks a frog to carry it across. The frog hesitates, afraid that the scorpion might sting it. Still, the scorpion promises not to, pointing out that it would drown if it killed the frog in the middle of the river. The frog considers this and agrees to transport the scorpion. Midway across the river, the scorpion stings the frog, thus dooming both. The dying frog asks the scorpion why it stung, despite knowing the consequence, to which the scorpion replies: "I'm sorry, but I couldn't resist the urge. It's in my nature."

I didn't understand then, but I responded to his story, "I'm a Scorpion." I was unable to stop myself from whistling through my teeth. I'd lost a couple of my baby teeth that summer. He nodded his head, pretending to wince at the sound - that high-pitched tone that happened whenever I said a word with an 's.'

"I know so many things about you, Charlie. I know you were born in November, which makes you a Scorpio, not a Scorpion, but I get your point, and I am happy to be your friend because I know all the wonderfully delicious things you will do."

He sat beside me while I lay on the bed and stared at the ceiling. The house's previous owner had painted a beautiful design around the light, with red, blue, black, and yellow swirls. Something from the 1960s, my mother had told me.

"Want to hear another one?" my imaginary friend asked, and thus, as he told me stories and as I tried to understand some of his references, another night passed.

When I first started school, I assumed that

3

everyone had a special friend that only they could see and hear. Luckily, he told me before I started school that not everyone had a friend like him. He also said Santa wasn't real for some kids. "For you, he's real, and I've talked him out of giving you coal this year. Although in the past, some of my friends would have thought coal a wonderful gift – fuel for heat. Your world has changed, Charlie, in so many unfortunate ways."

He often threw around clues and information about his past. When I'd mention him to my parents, they'd laugh a funny little laugh and tell me to get cleaned up for dinner or to get ready for school, changing the subject, as if having an imaginary friend like him was wrong.

But this friend's stories were amazing and he taught me a lot about the world and its corruption and all of the vile people, like my childhood nemesis, an evil boy named Johnny Fagan. Nobody called him by his given name; everyone called him 'The Fatman,' and unlike most kids who were overweight, he loved the title. Johnny Fagan thought of it as a royal title. He used his weight to his advantage when he played basketball, got into fights, or just tried to get his way by going belly first into a situation. He would pat his belly while talking to you just to let you know that if you messed with him, he would slam you against the wall with his belly first, and then he'd pull your hair and ears or punch you in the stomach which would make you double over feeling like you had to puke.

Whir watched me as I got ready for school. "He's got older siblings. That's the only way he would have this much training in torture. You know, I could have used someone like him in bygone days, but remember, Charlie, today is the day."

I looked at him, knowing what he meant, but I wasn't sure if I was ready. He scowled at me and added, "You'll take that knife with you to school today... don't put it in your backpack; your Mom will find it. Put it in your sock, but be sure you can get to it quickly."

As I pulled the knife out from between my mattress and the box springs, I asked, "Are you sure today's the day?"

"When have I ever been wrong? Now hurry, Charlie, your Mom's coming."

I quickly put the knife in my sock. The type of sock was not like today, not one of these tiny ones people wear. Maybe it didn't reach above the calf, but it did go halfway up, and the elastic could have leashed an elephant. I stood up, fixed my clothes to eliminate any wrinkles, and fixed my face, making sure not to think of the knife or to look down.

"Hurry, Charlie. I have to take your father his

lunch. He forgot it this morning," Mom yelled up the stairs.

Grabbing my backpack, I fell in line behind her, and we went through our morning routine. My life at home was always routine. There was no real excitement other than what I dreamed up with my friend. I saw Johnny as soon as we arrived at school. He was standing outside with a bunch of his friends. I bet today they would call them a gang, but back then, they were just hooligans.

He gave me the finger as I walked past. Kept it low so that no teachers would see and said under his breath, "You little freak, I'm going to get you today."

"Johnny, why won't you leave me alone?" I asked. I was genuinely curious, but his only answer was, "You know why." Neither my imaginary friend nor I knew. I was sure of this as I saw him shake his head. Both of us were wondering what Johnny was really talking about.

The morning was uneventful. I was still in grade school, and we had the same teacher for the entire morning and then a different one in the afternoon, with the classes separated by recess.

Outside, the sky was a deep blue. Dust from the baseball field was blowing across the playground, making everything hazy. Something felt off, and then behind me, I heard Johnny, "I'm gonna make you pay. I don't care if my Dad says he will tan my hide if I get into another fight. I'm tired of your bullshit. You shouldn't have told Miss Strickler about me."

Now, his saying bullshit was something of a novelty as well. Most of us knew the main curse words then, but Johnny was one of the few students who used them regularly.

"I'm going to hurt you this time, and it'll be so much worse than the last time. That's a promise, freak!" Johnny said while he clutched the back of my sweatshirt. As I took a quick step to get away, he kicked my back foot. I fell, luckily catching myself with my hands, but unfortunately, I scraped them on the asphalt.

He leaned down, and I could smell his breath. It always seemed to smell of baloney. He said through his yellow, crooked teeth, "After school, I'm going to catch you as you walk home and beat the shit out of you." Then he spat in my face.

We had stirred up a little commotion, but not too much. Johnny knew better than to make Miss Strickler have to stand up and walk over. She wasn't a small woman. Every fourth grader knew their hands would be sore by the time they wrote that they were sorry for whatever they had done five hundred times if she caught them being up to no good. She would even look at the words to make sure that the students hadn't taped two pencils together to try and make it go a little faster. She wasn't against cracking the back of their hands with a ruler either, though later, she would claim that she had been aiming for the desk.

I didn't hold anything against her. If I had to deal with all of the loathsome children she was teaching, I would have been the same. Luckily, I usually didn't incur her wrath. I'd smile my best smile, and she'd say, "Just be good, okay." It wasn't till later that I realized the sadness on her face every time she saw me smile, but that is a story for another letter.

She'd been a teacher at our little country school forever. "When they poured the foundation, I had to move, or they would have gotten concrete on my new dress," she used to say. Then she'd pat her dress and do a little turn, "See any concrete?"

I picked myself up, dusted off, wiped the spit from my face, and tried not to make eye contact with anyone. Walking over to Miss Strickler, I knew Johnny would be scared I was telling on him, but I didn't. I simply asked if I could go to the restroom.

I tried my best not to think of the knife in my sock. I started thinking about butterflies and kittens. My imaginary friend had told me, "When trying to get away with something or hide something, don't think of it. If you think about it, the universe will know, and the universe is a dick and cannot keep a secret."

At the time, I could barely understand half of the things he said, but this made sense. "You are my star pupil. You'll show them all someday."

Whistling through the hole left by my missing teeth, I went into the building, and instead of going to the bathroom, I went to Johnny's cubby.

I looked around to make sure that nobody was watching and pulled the knife out of my sock. A small folding knife with plastic grips. There was a small silverish whale on the front. My mom had almost caught me when I'd stolen it, but my imaginary friend had been keeping a lookout for me at the end of the aisle.

As you can guess, we'd been planning this for a while. "You have to stop him from bullying you, or do you want him to have a repeat of the incident, young man?"

I hated it when he called me that. He sounded exactly like one of those television dads, and I knew too well that they were all full of shit and sugar. *Sweet enough to make you want to believe in the stink that flows from their mouths,* I thought.

"No, no, no fuck, no..." I said the last bit under my breath, so Mom wouldn't hear us planning. I didn't want a spanking for using the f-word.

The incident? Sorry, but I will not tell you about

the incident... I'm sorry, Detective; there's no reason for you to know anything other than there was an incident that made it clear that when Johnny threatened me, he meant it.

Please, OK, NO, I won't talk about it... Fuck, stop thinking about it. I know you're reading this, wanting to know about the incident. I can feel you in the future wanting to know what happened to me. What caused me to be this way? While this didn't cause me to be what I am, it's an event I don't want to talk about. I don't want to tell you. You don't need to know about it. JUST STOP THINKING ABOUT IT! Please...

I'm sorry. Let me take a beat, and I'll tell you, but only this one time, and if I see it in the newspaper or on television, I'll kill everyone you love. I'll kill them all slowly. Spouses, friends, relatives, pets... I'll destroy everyone and everything you love, so DO NOT tell anyone.

I was happy on the day of the incident. I wore my new shoes. It was the first pair of new shoes I ever had. I'm not sure where my other clothes and shoes came from. Mom would see I needed something, and it would just appear on my bed the next day. We never went shopping like my friends and their moms.

The shoes had clued Whir and me onto this family mystery. I need you to understand. I seemed to have an endless supply of toys, all secondhand, and clothes that just seemed to fit perfectly whenever I needed them. When my Dad saw the new shoes on the table, he said, with a little sadness in his voice, "Guess not many trips to the attic left.".

Thinking back on it, I should have figured it out sooner. I knew that the attic would provide the answers I needed. I could barely contain myself the rest of the evening, thanks to the excitement about what I would find in the attic, but I was also a little nervous. Whir was surprisingly quiet as if he was worried for me.

"I'm ready, Whir. I think they're asleep."

"Not yet. Give it a few more minutes. Let's wait until the TV is off and your Mom has her earplugs in. It won't be long before your Dad's snoring drowns out the television."

"And the noise from the road, the airplanes, and the train as well don't forget," I added. Then I waited, not undressing for bed, and listened. When the television cut off, Whir said, "You'll need a flashlight."

I put my new shoes back on and went to the kitchen to grab a flashlight. A cold chill hit me as I moved back up the stairs. "We don't have to do this," Whir whispered.

He didn't have to whisper since only I could hear him, and his doing this freaked me out a little. Part of it was that he tried to blend into a situation. I guess his whispering reminded me to whisper to myself, "Don't worry. This is a fine adventure."

If I'd only known, I would never have gone into the attic. I almost stopped when I noticed how Whir was looking at me with a sad expression. He must have known what was coming, but he couldn't tell me. Usually, he was pale and had a shadow, like a cloak, that always hung around him. It looked cool when he moved. But right then, he just looked sad, and his shadow enveloped him like a blanket, not like a cloak or cape.

Walking up the steps, I paused and shut my parents' door. A chair with a flat seat stood against the wall. I'd seen my father stand on it to reach the rope to the attic ladder.

I moved the chair beneath the attic door and stood on it on my tiptoes, but I was too short to reach the rope. I took a deep breath, jumped, and caught the rope on my way down. I landed on the chair. The door came down a little as I pulled it, and caught the ladder, which slid out automatically.

"No rusty door sound," Whir stated the obvious and continued, "I was expecting more noise, but there's fresh oil on the hinges. Look," he swabbed a little on his fingers and held them under my nose to smell.

"Why keep the hinges oiled?" I asked Whir. But

if he knew why, he didn't say so; he just continued to look sad.

"We can turn back?" he warned me again. This was the second time he'd warned me.

I don't remember being afraid of anything, ever. I remember being sad, happy, and mad, and I have felt other emotions, but I've never been afraid. I think it's because Whir was always there to tell me it would be OK. He said he spat in the doctor's coffee after he saw him spank my bottom when I was born, but I don't remember that. I do remember that he didn't say I'd be OK if I went up to the attic, and I felt sweat run down the back of my neck.

I pushed the chair back against the wall and climbed up the stairs. At the top, I pulled the ladder back up. "No sense having one of them get up for a snack and find the ladder down."

It was pitch black in the attic. I could hear Whir beside me and felt his arm on my shoulder. It was comforting. He was shaking. *Scared,* I thought. Thinking back on it and what we would find, I imagine he was, but not scared for himself. He was scared for me.

I know now that he already knew the secret. He's a god of sorts and simply knew. I turned on the flashlight and shone it on Whir. For an instant, the light seemed to melt his face away, and I could see his skull and empty eye sockets. I blinked, and there he was again, my wonderful pale friend.

"We should go back. Let's go to the kitchen and get some ice cream." And there it was, the third warning. "There's power in three," he often said, and "A truth told two times can be a lie, but a truth told three times is the truth." As I mentioned, a lot of his words went right over my head, but as he gave me the third warning, I shuddered all the way to my core as if someone had walked on my grave. Imagine listening to a news story, Detective, about someone with your name getting killed. Yes, you'd know it wasn't you, but for an instant, you'd feel like I felt.

"No, I have to know." I turned the flashlight and shone it around. Shining the light across the attic floor, I noticed that it had a makeshift landing. I'd seen a house built by one of my neighbors, and they had rafters in the attic and just boards that were two feet on center. That, at least, is what I remember hearing them say. Don't know if that was true, but when they were on the ground, they were fun to balance on, and I tried to walk from one end to another, pretending I was trying to cross a lava-filled lake. A lot of kids of my generation worried about lava and quicksand.

The plywood floor was strong, and I felt comfortable walking around. Pointing the light straight ahead, I saw my reflection looking back at me. I almost dropped the flashlight, but it wasn't me nor a reflection. *A large picture of me?* I thought, walking closer to it. The picture hung on the far wall. Below it was a rocking chair I didn't remember seeing before. There was a spot in our living room where a rocking chair had once stood, but my Mom had never said what had happened to it. Beside the rocker was a small nightstand and a lamp.

Turning the lamp on, I could see the entire attic, and what I saw, well, I couldn't believe it. The picture was me and not me. It was someone who looked exactly like me. *My dad, when he was young. A cousin?* Yes, I know, Detective, you've already figured it out, but I hadn't. I was only in the fourth grade. Whir said, "He's your older brother. Andy. He passed away when you were little."

"I had an older brother? I can't remember him. Did you know him?" I asked, and the sadness returned to his face. But he didn't say anything. I looked around the attic and saw soccer, baseball, and football trophies. I even found a couple of Cub Scout badges.

"You ever wondered why your parents didn't let you go out for sports or join the scouts?"

The world was spinning, and I had to sit down on the rocking chair. I just sat breathing in and out a few times, trying to understand. How wonderful it would have been to have an older brother, Detective.

I thought of all the wonderful times we would have had.

There was a photo album on the stand. I wanted to see the pictures, but I couldn't open it. That would come later. I just sat rocking in the chair, thinking of how wonderful it would have been, and as I started to fall asleep, I realized that my parents had been lying to me all of my life.

I woke up in my bed the next morning... Well, in Andy's bed. Whir was not around, but I assumed that he'd carried me to bed. I thought about asking my Mom, but the way she'd been lying to me all my life, Whir and I agreed that she would keep on lying. Same with Dad. I ate breakfast, dressed, and with my new shoes on - *my shoes, they weren't Andy's; they were mine* - I walked to school.

The day was uneventful, but after school, on my way home, Johnny was waiting for me, "So, little turd, you need to pay tax to use this path."

"Screw you, Johnny." That was the first time I'd ever directly responded to him about anything. Usually, I'd just take it. He would come up with one of the schoolyard taunts about me sitting with someone in a tree, or he'd say that my mother sewed socks that smelled, and the ritualistic torture of youth would continue, but I was in no mood that day.

"Screw me? Screw me!" He jumped off of the log

he'd been standing on as if he needed any more help to look imposing and dove at me. Whir appeared and said something that I didn't understand, "Uppercut, scratch his eyes, elbow." But none of this registered.

Johnny knew his stuff. He kept everything to the body so that bruising would be minimal and I'd look like I'd just fallen. His buddies were around me, laughing, wanting me to scream or beg or something, but I didn't give them the pleasure. I took each blow, gritting my teeth, hoping that I would find a way to escape or fight back.

The attack didn't take long. Johnny was a lot bigger than me, and when I tried to get away, one of the others blocked my path. "Screw me?" Johnny bellowed while standing with one foot on my back. "Well, how about...?" and then he started laughing and wheezing. Asthma was his one weakness. It took him a few coughs to clear his lungs, and after a hit off his inhaler, he said, "Screw me... well, how about I piss on you?"

Taking a step back, he made a show of unbuckling his pants and unzipping.

"Turn him over," he commanded his crew, and they did. Thrashing around didn't help me get away, and I looked up at Whir for help.

"I'm sorry, but these are the lessons you must learn, but don't worry. His name will be the first on your list." Then Whir turned his back because he knew what was coming would be too painful to watch.

Three of them held me while Johnny stood on my left arm and started pissing on my face. I turned as best I could to prevent him from hitting my mouth, only to find that one of his buddies had the same idea. I will never forget the taste of their urine and the feeling of being helpless.

I'm not sure if I was broken then, Detective, but I was on the way to being broken. I know in today's society, an event like that could lead to drastic repercussions, but back in the day, we didn't know how much of a cesspool the world would become, so in the greater scheme of things, it didn't last long. Still, the memory of the assault haunted my dreams. Johnny threatened to kill me if I ever said anything, and then they were gone, leaving me soaked. I wasn't crying, though I wanted to. As I looked up, Whir still had his back to me.

I sat up and looked at my shoes. It was a miracle that they hadn't taken them and that they were dry.

Whir turned around and saw me looking at my shoes, and we both laughed.

"Well, you have that going for you," he said, "no pee on shoes, check," as if he'd been reading my mind. We continued laughing, and for the second time in as many days, he picked me up and carried me to the Nelson farm.

A creek passed by the farm, and as it was the beginning of September, the water wasn't that cold. I took off my shoes and jumped in, clothes and all. I did a little cannonball dive, not really sure why I was happy, but something in Whir's eyes had changed. I think I'd finally come of age.

When I got home, my parents told me they'd been worried, but they didn't pressure me when I said to my father, "Ever hear the story of the scorpion and the toad?" Whir whispered under his breath, "Frog." As always, they didn't hear him. I think something in my eyes scared my father, a glimpse of me knowing the truth. He quickly found something to do out in his shed.

The next couple of weeks were hell at school. My humiliation turned into an urban legend, with Johnny and his buddies saying at random times, "Man, I got to piss."

It was then that I asked Whir for help. "Whiro," I said, using his proper name and not just what I called him, "help me pay them back. Please." He smiled and pulled a notebook from the shadow that surrounded him. It looked new. I'd never seen it before. The words 'The Bloody List' were scrawled on the cover in an ink that was blood red and in cursive.

I couldn't read cursive very well, but I thought it

looked cool how the letters looped around. Opening the book on the first page, it simply read, "In life, evil lurks, and it must face retribution."

I turned the page and read the painfully clear, crisp penmanship.

1. Johnny 'Fatman' – Guilty of being a bully and harassing those around him.
2. ...
3. ...
4. Nick Holmes
5. Jason Holmes

The fourth and fifth were the names of Johnny's friends.

"What's the second and third with the two dots?" I asked Whir.

"Mom and Dad," he responded.

"What?" I was a little less shocked than one might have expected, but still, I was shocked.

"They're guilty. It's up to you whether you add them to the list or not. We can fill those in with others in the future if you like."

Well, I won't tell you my decision, but once we had the list, it was just a matter of planning the proper punishment.

Standing with a straight back, head held high, Whir looked down at me and said, "In the time before time, I had a job. I was tasked with the duty to punish those who were evil at heart. Liars, thieves, and those who didn't follow the true path. I was good at my job, Charlie. I can teach you now that you're ready."

That, Detective, was the incident. I hope you're happy that I told you. Please remember my warning. As you've seen, I'm good at killing and thoroughly enjoy handing out punishment to those who deserve it.

Now, where was I? Yes, I was in the classroom, knowing that recess would soon be over and Johnny would be the first in. He was, if anything, a creature of habit. I opened the knife, careful not to cut my fingers. Knowing it was extremely sharp, I turned it and smiled to myself as I slashed my arm and then stabbed myself in the side. Whir showed me where. Careful not to get blood on my hands, I dropped the knife inside Johnny's cubby.

I moved and hid beside the door to the playground.

"Hold your arm to your side so you don't leak on the floor," Whir advised.

We couldn't have planned it better. Almost as soon as I was in position, the door burst open, and Johnny ran past me without a second glance, turned the corner, and headed to his cubby.

"He's all about the snacks, that one is," Whir

whispered, as both of us had shared his Twinkies before I'd stabbed myself.

I knew that the others would be just a few seconds behind, so I walked back about halfway, and when the door opened again, I screamed and fell to the ground and delivered my line with perfect timing. Whir gave me the nod, and I yelled, "Johnny stabbed me."

Johnny dropped the little wicker storage box from his cubby, having come to yell at someone for stealing his snack, and the knife skittered across the hall.

You see, Detective, Whir and I have been at this for a long time, and you have no chance to stop me. You're on the wrong side of this. I'm handing down punishment from a god, maybe not your God, but a god nonetheless, and I've been at this for a very long time, even before you were born.

I will forgive what you've had the papers and news services say about me, 'quoting anonymous sources'. I know it's you, and yes, you did spark a reaction in me as you'd intended. In any case, I had planned to reach out soon.

I must also thank you for encouraging me to come forward to set the record straight, "White male, repressed tendencies, loaner, failure of a man." You have a lot to learn, and I promise I'll teach you. You see, I have been on a mission for a while, and I admit that I've grown tired, but my part in the mission is almost complete. My letters to you can serve as a warning to others in the future. "Be afraid; gods and vengeance await those not following the path."

I'll be mailing you more of these as I continue. I'll try not to spoil the ending for you by telling you how much longer I have to go.

On a personal note, I do want to say that I'm sorry to hear about your Mom's fall. I checked on her the other night, and she's doing well. I know that you were too busy down in Front Royal to check on her, and your worthless brother Joe is no help.

The doctor told me that her fall wasn't that bad. Luckily, she didn't break anything. I wish you'd have been able to be there. That nursing home she is in has issues, as you may have heard. I'm sorry you can't afford something better. I could try to send you some money, but I doubt you'd accept it from me.

Being a cop, you'll want to check her medicine. I think that one of the people at her home is stealing some of her pills; not sure if that was why she got dizzy and fell, but as healthy as she had always been, I don't think it was a coincidence.

I'm not sure who is stealing medicine or if, indeed, anybody is stealing medicine, but thinking about it, maybe I can try to find them and make room on my list for another name. As far as my mission being over, it seems I'm always finding someone who needs to pay. Whir mentioned there might be someone else joining the list soon.

I really liked your Mom. She reminds me of my Mother before I found out how evil she was. Was your Mom evil when you were younger?

I know I'm rambling. It's just so much fun talking to you, but it's time to go, Detective. Number 42 just pulled up.

2

A LIFE SO NORMAL

MILNER DAILY

THE ADONIS KILLER STRIKES AGAIN · MONDAY APRIL 12, 2010 · PRICE $1.25

Terrifying Message

Terrifying message from 'Adonis'. "Be afraid. Gods and vengeance await those who don't follow the path." When asked to comment, detectives had no explanation as to what not following the path entailed. The police ask the public to remain vigilant.

MONDAY, APRIL 12, 2010

Sorry, I cut the last message short. According to the news, you've been busy digesting the clues I left you at number 42's house... Did you get the joke? Come on, tell me you got the joke on digesting, as in dinner? The coroner will get it, but as young as he is, I doubt he remembers the scene in horror legend Vincent Price's movie. He played a character who used a surgical funnel in such a creative way. I admit that is where I got the idea. Well, Whir got the idea and reminded me of the movie. It was called 'The Abominable Dr. Phibes.' I'm not sure what year it came out.

It took several cans of the stuff, and the surgical funnel was tougher to find than I thought, but once she finally stopped moving around and it settled, it provided a very nice mold of the human digestive system. I do hope you put the picture in the newspaper. Have you seen where they pour cement into ant hills?

Whir says we're connected, you and I, sort of like the ancient Egyptian deity Apophis, the giant serpent of chaos and darkness that tries to stop Ra from bringing the dawn. He tells me that this is the reason why I can hear your thoughts when I close my eyes.

Whir has always given me strength and special abilities, but in return, he takes something from me. I'm not sure exactly how it works. It's hard to tell since he's been with me for so long.

You should know I like you, Detective, and I am impressed that you never asked, "Why Me?" That would have been the first question for some, especially in today's generation, which always feels sorry for itself.

So why you? While you weren't the lead detective on the 'Adonis Murders,' as the papers call it now, and yes, you did call me out with those comments, but the reason I'm connected to you is much simpler. You see, I'm you, Detective. Not exactly you, of course. The other side of the coin, perhaps, but you and I are the same. The only difference between us is that - I will paraphrase the Joker of comic book fame saying - "I've had a bad day."

Do you doubt that you would smite the world if someone did something to your kids? What if they did something to your partner? I know you've been together for a long time. You started as rookies together, I believe. Two female cops who found love on the beat. Tell me was she upset when you got the promotion before she did? I bet with her temper, she was.

Apologies, my brain meanders a little. I really want to tell you my story. It begins like all good stories... "Once upon a time, there was a replacement boy." Replacement boy, you wonder? You see, that is what I began to think of myself. I was a replacement for my brother, whom my parents couldn't take care of, so if, at first, you don't succeed, why not try again? I figured if the technology had been there and they'd have had the money, I'd be a clone, but they had neither the money nor the technology, so they did it the old-fashioned way.

Once upon a time, there was a replacement boy

who had to smite the evil bully. In addition to the knife with the whale on the handle, they found something in his denim jacket that looked like a joint. What were the odds that Johnny's older brother would have decided that 'Lil-Dude,' as he called him, needed his first joint that day? I bet that he'd planned on smoking it on his way home with his crew.

The police showed up, and the lead officer looked like a Greek god, arms stretching out of his short sleeves. I'd say he was a detective, but I really don't know if that's my memory playing tricks on me or not. Whir can't remember either, which is odd. He usually remembers all the details.

He's not with me right now. Between us, Detective, I'm beginning to think that Whir is becoming afraid of me. I've been talking to some of the other gods when he's not around, and they say he's worried about something. I wish I knew what it was.

I had been feigning unconsciousness when the lead officer came in, but I could see how powerful he was as he gave orders to my teacher and the principal. I'd never seen either of those two take orders from anyone. I'm older than you, Detective, but I still think we could have been friends. I don't say that to hurt or belittle you but just to set the stage for what the officer did next.

Johnny had been cowering on the floor, mumbling, "I didn't do it, I didn't do it." The lead officer picked him up by his shirt and slammed him against the plaster wall, sending bits of spittle and tears swirling through the air. It was quite beautiful.

Johnny – "I didn't do it."

Officer – "Mean to."

Johnny – "I didn't do it!"

The officer pressed harder on Johnny. I could picture his chest collapsing as the officer pressed his face next to Johnny and said slowly, "Mean to!"

Through my half-closed eyes, I could see Johnny squirming, and a wet spot appeared on his pants. Small at first, then larger as pee started to drip down his legs and onto the floor. Several kids who'd been trying to look out of their classrooms began to giggle.

The officer smiled and looked Johnny in the eyes. "I didn't mean to do it," and to my astonishment, Johnny repeated, "I didn't mean to do it."

"That's right, now take this punk out of here!" Officer Conrad said, thrusting him at one of the lesser-ranked officers. You know, the ones you look down on as they're clearing the scene for you to work. I see how you stride in, all-powerful and in charge. Most of the time, you do not even acknowledge them. I know you do talk to a few of them, some throwback to your days on the streets, but usually, you bark your orders and go in.

You doubt me, Detective. If you need examples, I'll email you some pictures and videos. You should be nicer to those underlings; most of them are decent people like you, and one is infatuated with you and your partner. This guy has pictures of the two of you from one of your softball games. You both look a little tipsy and are covered in sweat, with your uniform tops cut off, showing your bellies kissing. I like your belly better; not a fan of the belly piercing your partner has, but to each their own.

In the photo, her hand is in the middle of your back, and if he were to send that to one of the sports magazines, I have no doubt it would be a cover shot. To both of you, it's innocent, just celebrating the co-ed game you won, but to him, two women kissing is masturbation material.

Johnny ended up in a juvenile detention facility. Years later, he even came and apologized to me, if you can believe that. By then, following therapy, he was convinced that he'd been the one who had slashed and stabbed me. Isn't it funny how life pans out? This bully, who engaged in childhood pranks and treated me horribly, was brainwashed by the authorities into believing that he was capable of something like that. He's a preacher now. I check on him every now and then, and as long as he doesn't stray, he'll continue to live. He's still on my list, as are others who changed their paths, but Whir and I keep watch.

My parents saw me for the first time that day. I guess this was something that didn't happen to the other me, so they played the dutiful mother and father, asked all the right questions, and made sure I was taken care of.

Officer Conrad was there with me, asking questions. I worried that he could have some type of superpower, so I feigned ignorance of how the stabbing had happened exactly and focused on Johnny pissing on me with his buddies. I could see how angry he was getting as I played up the fact that Johnny was a lot bigger than me, and it worked. There was no doubt about my story, especially following Johnny's confession.

"If you need anything at all, kid. Here's my card."

I waited until after the stitches and staples had been taken out and gave him a call. True to his word, he helped me.

The rest of elementary school was uneventful. People who'd never talked to me before now asked how I was doing. They seemed to care. "They're faking it," Whir said. "They sense something different about you and are afraid of you, so you need to be careful."

When I got to high school and later junior college, my life was incredibly busy. Officer Conrad, later Sheriff Conrad, helped me as he'd promised, and my body changed in ways I'd never dreamed of. I had always been the small, skinny lad. But the Sheriff had me doing a lot of physical exercises and even suggested that I play football, "You've got some aggression in you, kid, and this will help channel it."

He was right; it did help, and over the next few years, I started seeing Whir less and less frequently. When I was having a moment of self-doubt, he showed himself, and we'd have wonderful conversations. He'd tell me about his travels, and I'd tell him things I'd been doing with Officer Conrad and how the team I was playing for at the time was doing.

I was a decent player, and it made me so proud to see Officer Conrad watching from the stands. You know, Detective, I'm not sure that my parents ever saw me play. They may have, but I'd begun a long time before just thinking of them as something functional, sort of like one's nose. It was there on one's face, and it held up your glasses, but other than when it's itching, you don't think about it. Now you're thinking about your nose itching... Sorry.

If there was food on the table, I'd eat. If not, I'd go to bed or my room and work on my homework or go to the gym. Officer Conrad had given me a key to the gym at the Sheriff's office. It was a lot better than the high school gym. He let me bring different team members, and we all took it seriously it was our private training facility.

My plans at the time were to go into law enforcement. I'd be a cop just like my father. Well, not my real father, but the only man in my life who really seemed to care about me.

We were both upset when I transferred out of state for college. It had been a tough decision, but we both knew it was best for me. I couldn't turn down the scholarship. We talked and planned for him to come out and see me play. The college had been scouting one of the players on my high school team, and it just so happened to be the best game of my life.

They offered me enough scholarships that I wouldn't have to work until school was done. Oh, did I leave that out? I had a job. You see, Detective, I was a junior deputy in charge of sanitation at the Sheriff's office at the time. I know, big fancy title to say that Sheriff Conrad hired me as a night janitor.

I was able to go in late after school and clean up. If there was a prisoner, I could get them a late-night snack or something to drink. Yes, under strict instructions not to open the door. By then, I was well on my way to where my muscles fit my frame. They still do, but back then, I packed on a lot of muscle, and with my martial arts training on the weekends to help with my balance, I wasn't worried about the prisoners in their cells, and I think Sheriff Conrad was more scared for them than for me. "You have to channel your violence."

We did have two famous prisoners who came through the jail. Do you remember the Belany Twins? John and Gabe had been charged with simple vandalism, but after the Sheriff searched their car and later trailer, they were guilty of way more than the original charges.

On the anniversary of his wife's passing, I almost told the Sheriff the truth about Johnny, but I didn't want him to think less of me. He was so sad, and I think that I wanted to distract him from that sadness, but I didn't. During the last six months of high school, I never saw Whir, and while I knew him to be real, I assumed he'd found another child who needed help.

On the first day at my new college, I was nervous while walking to my first class of the day. I had a lot of the same dreams as any college student. Would people like me? Could I handle the course load? You remember, I'm sure. What was your degree in? Oh, that's right, History. I walked up the hill from my dorm room to the main campus. The sun was rising, and I could barely see because of the light shining into my eyes. I'd planned to go to the gym, get a workout, and head to class. Shake off some of the nerves, if you will.

Through the morning haze, I saw shadows swirl around and could just make out someone beginning to appear in front of me. His name, Whiro, was on the tip of my tongue when she came crashing into my life.

I heard from the side, "Look out!" and turned quickly, making some moves that either looked cool or dorky. She'd never tell me and only smiled when I later mentioned how fast my reflexes had been. One time, I heard her say under her breath, "Just like Bruce Lee." Then we would have a tickle fight that I usually lost.

Her name was Kelly, and she was the one. To say that love slammed into me would be an understatement. Kelly had been trying out in-line skates for the first time, and she'd figured that there was less chance she'd run into anyone early in the morning.

The shadows disappeared as I caught her in my arms, turned, and somehow managed to keep both of us from getting badly injured. We fell to the ground. Her red hair was tied back into a ponytail. My arms around her in a quasi-lover's embrace, I looked into her deep blue eyes, and we started to giggle.

"First day?" I asked, but she must have misunderstood my question.

"First time." she answered, her words more of a

statement than a question before she continued, "No, I've fallen every time I've tried these."

"No, it's my first day on campus; thank you for the wonderful welcome. You knocked the funk out of me." Both of us kept laughing as we lay there.

She put her left arm under her head, my arm still under her back in our embrace, and asked, with a straight face, "So, you come here often?"

That was it. Detective, I wish I could have died at that moment. That was true happiness. Did you experience something like that with your partner?

I bet you did. The following months were amazing. I was so happy. Kelly and I were inseparable. She'd call me in my dorm room when we didn't stay together, and we'd leave the phones off the hook so we could hear each other sleeping.

I had told Sheriff Conrad about her that night when he asked how my first day was. He laughed and said, "Love is like that."

Over the next few weeks, life was perfect, and the Sheriff was planning on coming up to meet her before my first game. I wasn't going to play just yet, and freshmen usually didn't play on this team, but the coaches were impressed and told me to be ready. But I missed the game, and the Sheriff never got to see it. You see, one Thomas Everly had other plans.

Thomas had a heroin addiction. At least, that was what his lawyer said. That was why it wasn't his fault that he took the gun into the pharmacy. Thomas was dead, but his lawyer was still defending him.

The police report said that Thomas had been pacing back and forth, pointing the gun at anyone, demanding that the pharmacist stop the roaches. "They are coming out of my skin, look!" he yelled as he jerked in one direction, then another, unable to keep still.

Sheriff Conrad needed to pick up his blood pressure medicine, and being a creature of habit as police often are, he stopped at the pharmacy's back door and waved to Alice, the pharmacist's assistant. She was oblivious to what was happening out front and waved back while she continued to unpack boxes.

"His smile was so warm and friendly," she told the officer taking the report, "as if on Cloud Nine, without a care in the world."

As he stepped through the curtain, he told her, "I'm going to see my son Charlie..." He never finished the sentence. He saw Thomas Everly, drew his sidearm, and both men fired, the two shots sounding like one.

The pharmacist said, "We heard the Sheriff talking to Alice, and Thomas yelled, 'You called the cops?' I started to shout when I heard the Sheriff, but I was afraid. Sheriff Conrad dropped down to a shooter's stance and pulled his gun. Thomas, the gun in his hand, which had been shaking so badly, seemed to magically focus - his entire body stood still for this one moment. He'd been twitching so bad we had been afraid it might have accidentally gone off, but just then, he looked like something out of a movie, an assassin closing in on his victim. I couldn't see the Sheriff's hand. That's how fast he'd drawn his gun. Both shots rang out simultaneously. Both shots were true to their mark, and both men died instantly."

It made me so proud that he'd called me his son, Detective. What I can tell you, Detective, is that everyone I've punished deserved it. I would have killed Thomas a thousand times, but my father had taken care of him. Sheriff Conrad, that is. Later, when thinking about it, after Kelly was gone, I added his lawyer to my list.

Kelly went with me to Sheriff Conrad's funeral and only left my side for a moment to introduce herself to Mom and Dad. I saw them and nodded. Under my breath, I whispered, "I am not a replacement boy."

I felt someone touch my shoulder, turned, and saw Whir's cloaked face. He'd come to comfort me. "We'll make them pay," he whispered, but just like on campus, Kelly walked through him. She dissipated him, and her smile lifted me up. She brought purpose and light into my life.

Sheriff Conrad left me his house and his estate. That's a fancy way to say he left me his stuff. I had no idea about his will, what was in it, or how it would change my life, but with Kelly by my side, I had that hope of a future filled with dreams and memories of the wonderful man who lifted me up and gave me a life filled with joy.

3
PLAYING HOUSE

Friday, April 16, 2010

Kelly and I married shortly after college. She had a degree in computers, as she found early in life that she had a knack for them. She wasn't a master of anything but more of a generalist, and that suited her personality. She could go from one project to the next and never get bored.

I was in sales. The company I worked for was based in Leesburg, Virginia, and them, having been on the cutting edge of telework, allowed me a lot of freedom.

I don't think I missed one of my son's games or my daughter's plays. Or my other one... I won't tell you exactly how many kids, Detective. Let's just say I had the perfect life with 2.5 children, and I lived in a subdivision. I had enough money from the Sheriff's estate to pay off most of the house, so Kelly and I didn't go through the troubled years that a lot of couples do, stretching out leftovers for just one more night.

Kelly didn't care about expensive things. In fact, if I purchased something that cost too much, she would beg me to take it back if it was just for her, but for the kids, we gave them everything, and they thrived. If they wanted something special for their birthdays or Christmas, I'd say to them, "Well, you're only spending your inheritance, so it's up to you."

I remember one time when the youngest fell and broke her ankle. With recovery time we knew she wouldn't be able to be in the play she had worked so hard for. "I'm sorry I tripped, Daddy. I know you wanted to see me at the show."

She said this with such a big girl's voice that it broke my heart. I cried. Yes, me, Detective, a large man who still worked out, a little Dad bod going on, but that was okay. I tell you, I cried and wept like a baby. Holding her in my arms, she whispered, "Don't cry, Daddy, I love you, Daddy."

To which I responded, as I always did, "More than a bee sting?"

She giggled, saying, "Yes".

Then I added, "Ice cream?" and our little game of 'Do You Love Me More Than' would continue.

I need a minute. Be right back, Detective.

I'm back. You know, I still hear that when I shut my eyes. That little girl, who'd been crying earlier, was now trying to be strong for me. After she'd fallen asleep, I laid her on the bed and walked into the hall. Her older brother was there. Saw me and gave me a big hug, and he, ever being the one to take advantage of a situation, said. "She needs a puppy."

I leaned back, feigning surprise. I knew this was coming for a while. Kelly was behind him and gave a little nod as if to say, "She was okay with it if I was." I was elated, but I held it back and said, "She won't be able to walk it for a while. Will you?"

My son smiled, knowing that it was going to be yes, "Of course, I could even come back at lunch if you needed." I knew this last part wasn't something he really wanted to do, but being prepared to give up his freedom for his little sister was wonderful. You see, he'd finally reached the age where the students were allowed to go off campus for lunch. This was a big milestone back then.

"No, that won't be necessary, but we do have to make sure the puppy is hers. No plans for you to take it with you to college or anything."

"Okay, a family dog, but mainly hers and her responsibility," he shook my hand in agreement. A look passed between him and Kelly. I saw that were both grinning from ear to ear. I'd been duped, and I knew it when I heard a squeal, you know, the one. You have a daughter, that squeal of excitement when something they'd been wanting finally happened. With mock surprise that she had feigned sleep. I said in my big, best Daddy voice..., "Oh, you two set me up. Was your Mother in on this?"

I charged to the bedroom and started tickling my little girl as she squealed more with joy, and then she winced. I stopped. "Sorry, Honey, you okay?" She nodded, then I bellowed, "Daughter and Son of mine, I need a piece of paper. She has to sign, so she knows that Daddy owes her one tickle fight when she is better." My son gave me a little salute, you know, the way Jerry Lewis and other comedians would, and marched down the hall on his mission.

When Kelly came into the room, I smiled at my daughter, my voice devious, "Okay, miss good-little-girl with a hurt paw, was your mother in on it?" I held my hands out to tickle Kelly when my little princess squeaked out, "Yes, she was!"

Well, as you can imagine, lots of tickles went around, and even my son, who was 'too old' for tickling, got some.

"Now, you boys, go find a puppy and send pictures. We need approval, and if you find one, see if they can hold it till...," Kelly started and was cut off.

"No, Mommy. I trust Daddy. He will find the best

puppy in the whole world," my daughter blurted out in excitement.

"Okay, you heard her, now scoot. Someone needs a nap, and I don't mean the baby." Kelly came over and kissed me briefly on the lips, and that got the standard "Yuck and Gross" from all.

Okay, Detective, I only have two kids. No need to pretend. One boy and one perfect little princess.

There were a couple of shelters in town, so we tried those first. They didn't have anything, so I started calling the veterinarians. It didn't take long until I'd tracked down the most perfect, amazing puppy in the world.

He was at one of our neighbors' farms, a brown and white collie with long hair. "Your Mother won't like the long hair," I told him. He held the puppy, which was busy licking his fingers, while I drove us home.

Yes, I never called Kelly Mom, as some families do for short. It was Mommy or Mother, but never just Mom. That was what... well, over the years before we were married, Kelly tried to help me get closer to my parents; I'd told her how I had always felt like a replacement boy. I was sitting on the first bed that we bought together when she suggested having them over for dinner.

She was standing beside it, with her shirt off and bra on, and was not self-conscious at all. She knew how beautiful I always thought she was. She had the most beautiful physique of any woman I'd ever seen. We were planning on getting into bed, and I'm not sure why she said it, but a shadow must have crossed my face. She put her hands on either side of my face and kissed me, a kiss that seemed to last forever. Then she held me to her chest. I could feel her heart beating as she started stroking my hair and rubbing my back.

I felt tears run down my cheek and fall onto her chest. Later, when we're making love, I tasted the salt from the tears. I told her that I'd always felt like a replacement boy, and still felt like one to this day, that they still had not told me anything about my brother or his death.

I told her about Johnny and... well, what he had done and what I had done. I confessed all of my sins. Later, I was going to show her the notebook that I had, but I couldn't find it; *Whiro has it,* I thought, and he had not been on my mind since the Sheriff's funeral.

That night she held me so tight as we made love. I turned my face toward her chest, licking her nipples and moving my mouth up to her neck. I caressed her so gently and so lovingly. Kelly was my world then. I needed nothing else, especially not from my parents.

I remember standing beside the bed, deep inside

her, hearing her moan out my name as we both climaxed. Her breasts looked so warm and inviting as I collapsed on top of her, both of us giggling when I pulled out, and we said, "hate that part," in unison. The separation, we were one and then separate and alone.

I lifted her to the center of the bed and laid down beside her. With her head on my chest, I wanted to feel all of her love. Kelly pulled my face to hers, kissing me again and again, her hand lovingly resting on her belly, "You'll be such a great Daddy,"

The puppy was a giant hit. It took to my daughter and would chew, I mean fetch her shoes. I'd hear my her giggling at night as the puppy would be licking her toes or face, and in my daddy voice, I'd yell "That puppy better be in his crate." To which I'd hear more giggles and a mocking response, "He is." I'm proud to say, Detective, that I've never used my daddy voice in anger.

A few more years passed, and just before my eldest was to go off to college, Kelly's parents were supposed to come visit. But something happened to my father-in-law's back, so it was decided Kelly would drive up with the kids the first week school was out, and I'd follow that weekend. Sport, who turned out to be my dog in the end, stayed with me. He was still a family dog, but all of the duties of dog ownership had fallen to me. The kids being in school, he just sort of took to me, and we waited together for everyone to come home. We both would greet everyone with the same enthusiasm when they returned home. Our only desire in life was to be with the ones we loved.

Kelly's Dad was allergic to dogs, and we thought it best if I brought him up with me. "Sport can sleep in the pool house with you," Kelly told me.

"As long as you visit like you did when we were in college," I responded. Though both kids were older, we still got the same "Yuck, Gross" from them, and my princess added, "Get a room."

Why didn't I go earlier? Well, it was partly the dog, but also my work. Our numbers for the quarter were not where we wanted them, so I needed to work. One of my clients promised me a big sale, and there was no chance for me to take off early. I'd have finished it remotely, but the Internet up there was horrible back then, so I stayed home. Waving at them as they pulled out, I didn't notice the dark shadow that passed between us as I turned to go inside. You see, he knew, Detective. Whir knew and didn't tell me.

How many times have you told your spouse or children that you can't do something because you're on a case, Detective? I hope that I've not caused you to work too much overtime. I try to keep busy with planning over the weekends, so as to not call you out late, but I know it's happened. I've thought about calling it in so that someone finds the bodies right after I'm done, but with as many cameras and technology these days, I'm worried someone would catch me using one of the few pay phones left in this city. That's why I don't, and for that, I'm sorry.

I'm nearly done with my list. I've been working on it for a while; forty-two from the other day was fun, but just know, Detective, I'm not working on them in order. There are people on that list, like Johnny, whom I may never have to punish. After I'm done with the active ones, I may just go away. Let Whir take care of them. I'll move to Belize, or an island paradise, maybe tour the Mayan ruins, or something. Kelly and I always talked about that, but we never had the time. I believe that Whir is from there, or at least he used to be worshiped there at one time. I've seen carvings that look like him.

When you were an officer, did you ever have to knock on a parent's door? That must be the worst job in the world. It wasn't something I ever had to do. The Sheriff did it for everyone in our small town, whether he was on duty or not. The weather had been good, but there'd been an accident.

"A horrible accident, a freak accident. Really no one's fault," well, that was what they told me while I petted Sport's head. As I'd mentioned, he was basically my dog. When Sport was a puppy, he followed my princess around like a good dog. I remember one time she painted his toenails. She'd been practicing, and he looked at me like, 'Aren't you going to do something with your kid?'

A couple of times, both mine and her brother's nails were done up nice and pretty. Well, as good as she could do them. She had trouble with coloring as well, she did not like to stay within the lines. My son made her swear to never tell anyone. She was the princess for all of us, and we all felt love every day.

Kelly and I took some martial arts classes. It was something fun to do together; it kind of became our date night, and she was no help as I tried to explain to the martial arts class why my toenails were candy-apple red. Our instructor smiled, he knew my daughter well, and told us, "That's why I always wear shoes around her."

As little girls do, they change priorities and get interested in boys, teen idols and other things. Parents and dogs stay behind, praying they come home safe.

I knew a couple of the officers that came by. We talked about the Sheriff, and they made sure that I was OK before leaving. "If you need anything, Mr...." Oh wow, that would have been silly to put my last name there.

I looked around the empty kitchen. I wanted to remember what the last meal we had eaten together was, but I could not remember. I just didn't know, and Detective I also didn't know what to do.

Yes, I knew that I needed to go to the hospital, but for the first time in my life, I didn't know what to do. Kelly wasn't there, and I had no one to ask other than Sport. I heard a low growl as a shadow passed by the fridge, and there was Whir. "I'm sorry to hear about your loss...," he started.

I screamed, "Fuck you, you aren't real! Get the fuck out of my head!"

"You have no idea what I am," he whispered, but as Sport moved forward, he retreated and, like that, was gone. I had heard that the Chinese use dogs to chase spirits away, so maybe that was why Whir left.

I called the police station and asked if they could talk to the police in Pennsylvania and send someone to her parent's house. I asked that they let me know when they were close, and I would call. I just wanted someone there to comfort them.

The sound of a parent crying out when notified of a child's and grandchild's death is one I that I hope to never hear again. I told her father, who was, in my opinion at the time, the stronger one. The police came to the door, and there was more crying and, "What happened?" To which I said, "Don't worry, I'll take care of them."

I'm going to have to go now, Detective. Just

know that we're in this together, you and I. Oh, Sport? He's doing fine. I gave him to Kelly's parents. It was almost as if Sport knew he needed to be with them for a while. I purchased a farm a little while ago in Wytheville, Virginia, and when I finish my list, Sport and I will retire there. While Belize is beautiful and could be fun, Sport is old, and being a long-haired dog, he would not enjoy the heat.

Kelly's father, whom I knew had taken a lot of allergy medication, just hugged the dog and wept. When I offered to have Sport stay with them for a while, they both loved the idea—not a replacement, but something to comfort them. Maybe that was how my parents thought of me. Or maybe I was just an unhappy accident that reminded them of my brother.

Detective, What do you think? I am sorry, but I have to go. I'm enjoying our talks. Tonight's number is 312, just pulled into her driveway. I added her to a spot on my list that I had been saving for someone else. As I said, she was stealing her medication. I figured you wouldn't have a chance to investigate. 312 has made a lot of money selling patients' different medications. I am going to leave you a gift with this one, I hope you like it.

4
SAYING GOODBYE

MILNER DAILY

NURSING HOME SAVIOR? — MONDAY APRIL 19, 2010 — PRICE $1.25

Nursing Home Savior?
by Natalie Russell

Several of us are wondering about Adonis, the so-called Serial Killer's motivation and with the latest victim is he a Savior or a Killer?

Detective Martinez's mother was a Shady Pines nursing home resident and a victim of medication theft. M.S. Martinez could not be reached for comment, but an anonymous source told this reporter that a nurse

Medication Theft on the Rise
by Ron Stead

A study by the National Institute of Justice found that 1 in 10 nursing homes had experienced medication theft by staff in the past year.

The average value of the medications stolen was $1,000 per incident.

The theft of medications can have serious consequences for residents, including

Police Keeping A Lid On Emails...
by Kent Green

The police have not been forthcoming about how the electronic messages are being sent. The emails as they are frequently known "Can usually be tracked," one IT resource told this reporter.

Is the Adonis killer smarter than the police, or simply lucky. That is yet to be determined.

MONDAY, APRIL 19, 2010

I wonder what you think of me, Detective. How many bodies have you found? Did you think I was a man, a woman, or something else? I bet you initially thought I was just your average psycho. And now, do you think I'm a murderer?

I know that you are glad that your Mom's getting all of her medicine. Did you know how much of a problem medicine theft is in nursing homes, statistically speaking? They don't track it, but I read somewhere that over twenty-five percent of nursing homes report missing controlled substances. Anyone who takes from the helpless like that is no better than hyenas scavenging off the dead. They should pay for that, but I'll leave the others up to the authorities, and who knows, maybe Whir and his next friend will do something. It's hard to believe how many criminals there are in this world who take from the helpless, It makes me sick.

In your Mom's case, I think it was just this one worker stealing her medicine late at night. I would keep an eye on your Mother for you, but I saw that you moved her someplace else. A new facility? A relative? One of those Angel services that offer home visits?

It really doesn't matter to me. I just wanted to give something back. I feel that our relationship has grown so strong over the last few years since you've been on my trail. I did get a kick out of Officer Benjamin's theory that I'm part of some type of satanic cult. Haha, there's nothing that could be further from the truth - now you know why I'm writing to you and not him.

Oh, Whiro? Well, yes, he claims to be an ancient god, but he's not Satan, and other than him having prior knowledge of some things when I was a child. I don't know that he is supernatural. Thinking about it, I could guess it is a dissociative disorder. But that is for another day. He's looking at me now as I write. I wonder... does he know I've added him to the list... I just looked up and smiled at him, looked him in the eyes for a long time, and wouldn't you know it... he blinked first. I think there is a quote about looking into the face of hell.

The night I was notified, I went to the hospital. Packed up the dog, and since I'm a planner, my bags for the trip were already packed. I did not think I would need the sunscreen, but I just kept it packed as it was. Even the condoms. Yes, I'd packed condoms a few months before. My wife had a lady problem, and she had to go off the pill for a while, so there we were, at our age, buying condoms again. She made me go to the drug store, and dammit if I didn't feel like a teenager, and all of the self-checkout lines were full. There I was, the father of a high school senior, standing in the queue, trying to not let Mr. Ramport see me buying condoms. It was funny how crazy and nervous I felt. I wondered if it was a generational thing. I know it must be a guy thing. You women are a little more civilized; well, that's me being a generalist. My wife was more civilized, I should say, and things like that she just takes... took in her stride. Now I bet I could just pull up the pharmacy app and have the condoms delivered.

Sport and I drove to the hospital. Calling ahead, I found out from the receptionist where I needed to go to identify them and make arrangements. As it happened, the arrangements were the easy part. Kelly's mother had always wanted to have all her family together in the same graveyard and purchased enough plots for our kids, my wife and even for me. She'd planned it out, so even if we'd had a dozen kids, we'd be in the same plot.

"If you hurt me, Mom and Dad will take away your grave," Kelly used to say and laugh, and I'd reply, "I'll get cremated and have someone pour my remains over your grave so I'll be on top of you for all eternity."

Then my boy, ever the jokester, said, "You know, I bet Grandpa has a leaf blower."

You would have loved them, Detective. They were real and genuine and there wasn't a mean bone in their bodies. I knew something about myself ever since the incident with Johnny and made sure that neither my son nor daughter would ever be like me.

I had confessed to Kelly about Johnny and at the time, I was scared that it would be the end of us and that my evil would be passed down to the kids. Holding me, she said, "I love how you are." And I wish now that I'd said what I thought instead of just kissing her. I should have told her the entire truth and said, "But you don't know all of me. You don't know that when I close my eyes, I see red. I see a blood red rain and it pools all around us, and it makes me... and it doesn't make me sick. It excites me." Maybe she could have helped, or maybe she would have gone back to her parents and taken the kids. They would still be alive. But as it was, the thought of the blood rain excited me and made me so aroused. I started kissing her, and we made love. I wonder whether she wondered why I kept my eyes shut, just imagining the blood like rain pouring down on us. It was simply a beautiful moment, Detective. I'm getting hard now thinking about it, but now's not the time. Where was I? Yes...

The hospital was one of those giant medical centers, like the one in Winchester, with different buildings and offices. The receptionist gave me good directions, but I got turned around several times. Sport was sitting on the seat beside me, his head in my lap, and as I rounded the corner, I saw several news vans and an officer waiving me on a detour.

I flashed my badge. Oh, yes, I am still in law enforcement. You may have guessed, but don't worry, I'm not a full-time officer. I help out occasionally at a parade or event, and before the Sheriff passed, he made me a badge-carrying volunteer. I did have to go through the same police academy, and it was so much fun. I thought of becoming an officer, but when the Sheriff died, I didn't think it would be as much fun. I know it would have been cool to hang out with my real Dad.

"I need to get to..." then, looking at the paper I'd written the directions on, I continued, "The Mayton building. My family was in an accident."

The officer's face gave a brief knowing look. Evidently, everyone on the force there knew about the Mayton building. Being from out of town, I didn't have a clue, but seeing the officer's look, I had the feeling of someone stepping on my grave. Officers of the law are willing to put their lives on the line for anyone. All they ask from the universe is that they can come home after work and find their family safe.

"I'm sorry, Sir. You can cut through here. I'll waive you through. Otherwise, it's a shit show navigating around. The media is here, so you may want to wear a hat as you walk in. No need to give the vultures a show."

"Thank you, I hadn't heard that it was something that would be newsworthy."

"The Governor's son...," then he paused and rethought what he was going to say, "Yes, I think there was someone related to the Governor, and you know he's in a tight race to stay in office. Anyway, the media is trying to see if it was more than just an accident and they're looking to get photos."

"Thank you, and I understand. I just want to get my family and take them home."

"I'll radio so they clear you to park..." A short bark interrupted him. "Well, hello, I didn't see your pup there. Beautiful dog," he continued, to which Sport barked a response. But Sport wasn't barking at the officer. He was barking at Whir, who was walking past the officer unnoticed. I assumed he was on the way towards the building where... well, towards my family.

Parking, I could see all of the news vans and even saw M.S. Ellie A. Remember her? She came over asking if I was a member of the family. "No, Ma'am." I stretched out my southern drawl as far as I could, "I'm just on the cleaning crew. Forgot something when I left. What's up?"

Ignoring me since I wasn't part of the story, she said, "Okay, sorry to bug you," and turned away. "James," she yelled into her earpiece, "get setup over there. I want to cover the families as they come in. Wait... is that Liam, Liam, Liam, Ellie A from..." I tuned her out but followed her gaze to a man about thirty. Later I found out he was Liam Pratt, the aforementioned Governor's son. Having worked a little in law enforcement, I saw that he was very intoxicated. His arms moved like they were made of jelly.

An officer quickly stood in front of the camera.

"I'm sorry, you'll have to give the families room." And then the officer pointed at me, "Miss you're blocking family access, now let him through."

Well, I was busted. She knew that I was family, and the questions started. "Did you vote for the Governor? You're the father. How come you weren't with your family?"

It was the last one that got me. Before that, I'd been trying to watch Liam, but she made me lose track of him. Turning my back on her, I opened the passenger door and said, "Spike, kill." I had spent a lot of time with Sport over the years, and the 'Spike, kill' phrase was my way of saying he could tackle the person in front of him to lick them to death.

Now to my knowledge, Detective, no one has ever been licked to death by a dog, but seeing him dive out of the truck and bounding at her was just great. She stumbled backward and fell, scuffing her hands on the asphalt. "Heel," I said, and Sport being a good dog, did a 180 and fell in beside me as we walked into the Mayton Building.

A security guard asked who I was as I walked up. He was laughing; evidently, he didn't like Ellie A either, but he looked at Sport as if to say he couldn't come in. I flashed my badge, "He's a working dog, and he deserves the chance to say goodbye to his family." The guard's smile turned into a frown, and while he didn't meet my eyes, he simply nodded as he let us pass.

At the reception desk, Sport did his job. He went around to the side of the desk and said hello to everyone. Sitting in front of them one by one until they petted him and said either, 'Good dog, or Beautiful dog.' He accepted other compliments, turned, and came back to me.

"Our family is here; We'd like to see them."

They took us to a small room to wait. I knew they were trying to get everything as ready as possible, to make the dead presentable, if you will. Sitting there, I remembered waiting for my wife to get ready. Even on our wedding day, she was late. "Mommy's still getting ready," was something that my kids and I said a lot; I said it now to Sport, adding, "We have to say goodbye."

In the next room, I was shown three forms under sheets, their faces covered. "Do you want me to stay?" asked a preacher-looking male nurse. I didn't really think he was a preacher, but he might have been. He had very soulful eyes and a caring face—someone you would entrust your most prized possessions to, and I guess I was.

"No, we would like a little privacy if that's allowed."

"Of course. Shall I lower the sheets?" he asked.

"No, I'll do it. Thank you for taking care of my...,"

I couldn't finish. The words just wouldn't come out. I lowered my head and felt Sport leaning closer against me. On the trip, he'd sensed something was wrong, and now he knew that our worst fears had come true.

As I lowered the first sheet, the door closed behind me. It was my wife, Kelly. I'm not sure what I'd expected, Detective. I could feel a shadow circling my soul and could tell that it wanted me to rage, that it knew. That Whir knew who'd done this and that they had to pay, but I pushed all of that down when I heard Sport give a little growl. Sport and I both knew that I needed to focus on my family for the last few minutes that I would ever see them.

Shaking my head, I said, "I love you to infinity." I gently kissed Kelly on her mouth. That phrase had been a running joke with us. I'd say, "I love you to infinity," and her response I could hear in my ear then, "Well, I love you to infinity and back."

I found her arm under the sheet and held her hand down so that Sport could smell and lick her hand for the last time. "Dogs don't feel loss," I've heard people say, well, that's bullshit. Mine did.

Next, I went to my son's body. Such a big strong boy. The officers at the house said he'd been the last to die. He'd died in the hospital. They thought he was going to make it. Later I read the police report. He'd been screaming for them to get his mom and sister and leave him. He'd been thrown from the vehicle, and they'd found him trying to crawl back to get them out.

My princess, I can't tell you about her and what I did or said, Detective. Maybe when we meet, and we will meet, just know that... I just found it hard to say goodbye.

Sport and I stood there, unsure what to do with ourselves. Where to go? There was nothing more I had to do in my life. Being someone who worked all the time for my family, I was at a loss of what was to come next.

I said, "Watch," and Sport, ever the dutiful dog, turned, laid on the floor, and watched the door. If he heard something, he would huff, not bark. What a good dog.

When I was training him, Kelly asked. "Why don't you want him to bark?"

"Because I want whoever is coming in to come, but I don't want them to know we're ready."

Kelly would say "You're a goofball!"

The kids would start saying in unison, "Daddy's a goofball,"

My Princess would ask, "What's a goofball?".

Oh, how I loved them.

I pulled all three sheets down, then I took in all of the damage, every twisted bone, every gash, every puncture wound, every scratch, everything. They'd cleaned them up the best they could, but I took it all in. Forcing myself to start at the top of their heads and look all the way down to my Kelly and my Princess's painted toes.

"We have to match at the pool, Mommy," she'd had said before leaving. She was so mature in a lot of ways, but when it came to painting her nails, she seemed to revert back to when she was little.

I stared at them, Detective, making sure that I'd never forget. Maybe if I'd left after saying goodbye and not pulled off the sheets, my path would have been different, but I needed to see the damage. I needed to see how much someone needed to pay.

I heard Sport make a sound and then whimper behind me. I heard Whir say, "Never forget. You saw Liam. Saw them hide him from the news media."

He wouldn't fully come into the room, because of the dog. After he finished speaking he turned and left. I think he knew then, that someday I would kill him. He left through the wall; all I saw was a trace of his shadow as it disappeared.

Sport looked at me, but he didn't bark, just gave a little chuff sound.

"Good Boy. We'll go soon."

I covered them back up, brushed my Princess' hair a little, and allowed Sport to sniff and lick their hands one last time.

Outside, it was a circus. More news crews had

arrived, but M.S. Ellie A didn't come near me as I exited the building. Once in the truck, I looked around, but I didn't see Liam.

Detective, this has been hard for me to write. I hope you understand that. I'm going to take a week or two off. I know it's your eldest kid's birthday, and you've had plans to take your family to that magical place... Please go ahead. I'll not be visiting anyone on my list for the next three weeks. I promise, one officer to another.

5
LIAM'S FALL FROM GRACE

Monday, May 10, 2010

I didn't go after Liam right away. I knew that he was guilty, but I gave the legal system a chance to work. I'd even called the tip line for Ellie A. Figured I kind of owed her one for the scare, but as you know, justice is slow sometimes.

The next few months were a blur. I spent a lot of time cleaning. Not sure why, but I became obsessed with making sure there was no dirt at all in the house. The only things I didn't touch were my son's, wife and daughter's toothbrushes. Kelly never once put the toothpaste back, the cap on it, or her toothbrush away. I swear, Detective, there were times I'd find it on the couch because that was where she was when she'd finished brushing them. "At least the kids keep theirs in the bathroom... Most of the time."

I'd joke. They'd inherited that habit from their mother.

The only announcement I saw on the news and then later read in the paper was 'No charges filed in the accident on route...' The newspaper article went on to say that the cause of the accident must have been related to faulty tires on the family's car and the weather.

I'll admit I was bad when it came to maintenance on my truck, but when it was my wife's SUV, I was a stickler, and everything was good. The next day I went up to the police station, and the only thing of interest I saw were the bumper stickers for Governor Pratt on several of the officers' personal vehicles.

Still trying to follow the rules and do things as Sheriff Conrad would have wanted, I asked to see the Sheriff. I had to wait a long time, but when I was finally able to get to his office, I learned where the officers got the bumper stickers.

There were stickers, buttons, and other campaign materials for Pratt throughout the Sheriff's office. One even said, 'Sheriff Elder says, VOTE Pratt'. I asked why Liam hadn't been charged, but instead of anything even remotely sincere, I got a lecture. "While you were waiting, I called your department, and they said you were part-time but hadn't been in for a while. Our Governor is a powerful man in this community, you know." I don't know what type of veiled threat that was, but I took it in my stride.

I didn't mention that I'd seen Liam out front that night. That he was weaving back and forth. I had recognized two of the officers in the outer office who'd been holding him up, and another one I'd seen give him coffee while I was dealing with Ellie A.

I didn't bother going to see Ellie A. As I was driving home, I heard a commercial for her show, "Tonight, on Ellie A., a one-on-one with Governor Pratt."

You see, Detective? Everyone sold out. Each of them got something they wanted out of it, while my family was six feet under. I stopped at one of the electronic stores and picked up a couple of laptops, tablets, and other electronics I'd need, keeping my hat pulled down to cover my face. I figured if they ever got a picture, I might as well look the part. I paid in cash.

Had I been planning this? Not really, but I admit that I am the type of person that runs through different scenarios before acting on different impulses.

"Would you like to be a rewards member?" the lady behind the counter asked.

"No, I can't even spell computers. These are gifts. Can I get a gift receipt?"

She whispered back, "I can't spell it either, Hun."

Once home, I started doing some research. No research on Liam or his father. For that, I'd go to a coffee shop. I'm sure you know anyway, but when it was my wife's SUV, I was a stickler, and everything me, "They can track you online." I researched a few hacking sites that I'd heard her mention. She'd always been good at computers and cyber security, and I knew the basics and at that time, the biggest thing was to not be afraid of them. I'd never had an interest or desire to go deeper. It didn't take long. You can learn how to hot wire a car and get stains off a kitchen counter on YouTube.

The next day I drove a town over, found a doughnut shop that had free Wi-Fi, and started my search in earnest. I reached out on a couple forums and chat rooms. I was trying to find out where the fun people hide on the deep web.

Just in case someone tracked me back to the shop, I kept my face from directly facing the cameras in the store. I paid in cash and I wore a fisherman's hat that said, "Forgot Bait? I have a worm." Memorable, but just the hat, not me. The electronics of the day weren't up to where they are now, but even then, I didn't have a cell phone while traveling, and I shut off all of my electronics for the trip and turned off all the location services.

My truck was built before GPS and was, well, technically, Sheriff Conrad's. We just kept paying the bills every time they came in and didn't bother changing the name on the registration. You'd think that the DMV would catch it, but they never did.

You may think I was taking a lot of unnecessary precautions for this research, and you'd be right, but I wanted to start developing good habits. I carried my notebook with me every place I went. You remember the one with the cover that said, 'The Bloody List'. I'd found it after they'd died, right where I'd left it. I was surprised at the number of names already in it.

I had a few people look at it when sharing a table at a coffee shop, but I told them, "I'm an indie horror author. Do you like to..." and most times, people's eyes would glaze over, and I would be left to my research.

As I said when opening the notebook that first time in the doughnut shop. I saw way more names than I'd remembered writing. Johnny was number one, a question mark by his name, with those two blank spots left for my parents. I flipped a few pages and then added:

300. Liam Pratt – Guilty of murder

301. Sheriff Elder – Guilty of conspiracy to cover up murders.

302. Governor Pratt? – Did he know?

303. Ellie A – Guilty of conspiracy to cover up murders.

I thought about the deputies, but while guilty of helping to sober up Liam, they were acting under orders from the Sheriff and possibly the Governor.

I used all the traditional search engines before I moved to some that I knew from law enforcement, tracking down Open-Source Intelligence (OSINT). It's amazing what information is in the public domain, if you only know where to look.

Using different variations of his name, I found that Liam had joined several dating sites. He used the same photo for his dating profiles as he did on his public social media profiles. It looked like Liam was into fast cars, and one type in particular. "Nothing's as amazing as this in red," one of his posts said.

I found him on the more popular dating sites. I created a couple of different profiles. I wasn't sure what type of catfish this guy liked, but I'd find out soon.

Profile - Suzie Q. Looking for someone who likes their cars fast and their women faster. Just need a little help.

Profile – Jesse A. Looking for a Daddy to teach me. Help me get through some tough times.

Profile – BlueEyes – If you have to ask, you can't afford me.

I went on some other sites as well, some of the freaky sites dedicated to bondage and discipline, dominance and submission, sadism and masochism

(BDSM). Part of me wished that I'd found this scene while my wife was alive. She'd been creative and might have enjoyed the costumes. As it was, I put up a few profiles of submissive types. Liam would think himself dominant.

Detective, have you ever been on any of those sites? Kind of depressing, if you think about it. Lonely people looking for other lonely people, all trying to find that love of their life or that quick fix for what they're missing at home.

The photos I'd picked for the women all looked like the types I'd seen him with on social media and on the news. I was trying to understand his tastes. I even had a few that looked like a younger version of his mom. While I waited, it was exhausting seeing how many lame guys were on those sites with their intro lines. I loved and missed my wife, but I didn't think that I'd ever find love online.

The first few days, I didn't have anyone that looked like him, so I went to a different coffee shop and tried again. I changed town each time I changed coffee shop. Not doing a circle of my town, but more a triangle, and then another triangle along the edges.

It was just before closing one night when the manager said, "Sorry, mister, about thirty minutes to go. Okay? Need another coffee? It's on the house. I have to empty out the pot."

"Thanks, but no, I'm good. I drink coffee now, I'll never get to sleep. Go back to college, they said to earn a degree..." I let my words trail off as I looked back down. Taking on the persona of a man trying to get some education late in life.

A chat request from Liam appeared on the computer screen. Or someone that looked like Liam and used one of his emails that I had found.

"Hi, you need help?" That was his message.

As you can guess, he was the type that wanted to be the hero, to rescue the girl, to take her away from her boring life for a few minutes.

"Can't talk now. He's almost home. Can we chat tomorrow night?" I wrote.

"Please, baby, we can talk till he gets home. What are you into?"

"Anything that gets me out of this trailer. Oh, shit, hang on." I typed.

Then I waited. I didn't have much time, but I wanted him to squirm, and he texted a few emojis of the fingers tapping until I responded, "Good news, he has to stay at the fire station tonight." I typed, figuring that any chance to stick it to a fireman, as they say, would be good with him, what with his father being on the Sheriff's team.

"That's great news, baby. Let's meet. I need some good loving, do you swallow?"

I had to stare at the computer for a second. This

guy couldn't really think that would work. But what the hell?

"Why don't you come here and find out? I can't leave the house. He takes the keys when he goes. Have to protect my property. That's how he puts it. Can you come by and leave me a little help after? I'm trying to save up so that I can get out for good. Maybe when I do, you can drive me, and I'll be your good girl."

We went on for about ten more minutes, and I gave him the address and told him to give me half an hour so that I could be ready for him. "Do you want me to shave? Hehe," I typed at the end.

"Yes, please, I so need that. Wife's a fucking forest down there."

I dropped the connection and started the laptop's self-erase function that I'd programmed into it. Basically, I watched it reboot, and the formatting of the hard drive started. Not quite to military spec, but who would know to search for it? Outside, I walked to one of the donation boxes. Keeping my face away from the camera, I took a couple of alcohol pads and put on some disposable gloves. Gave the laptop a good wipe and dumped it in the donate box. It was supposed to be for clothes and shoes, but I'd seen some other things in there.

I figured that would be a nice surprise for

someone coming to donate clothes. Would they keep it or not? Did it matter?

When I started this, I looked for places to rent, and I have a few in Virginia. Even one in.... Well, I'll get to that later. I rented them in different people's names from my notebook and several variations of Liam's name. My wife's company had a good life insurance policy I didn't know about, and her planning for eventualities had upped it to its maximum and made it possible to keep several properties running at once.

Inside the trailer I'd rented, I had the scene already prepared. The trailer had been set up as a hunting cabin. It fit my purpose - it was remote and had utilities. When I'd talked to the owner, he'd told me, "You can hunt year-round. I'm a farmer, I've got the right to thin the herd."

I had no desire to correct him on the law not applying to us renters and told him I'd check it out the next time we'd be in town. "If we like it, I'll just leave the money for the next two months on the porch."

With a nervous laugh, I continued, "I think I may need to kick my brother out for snoring if the place is small." I picked up the keys a week later, making sure that no one was there. I searched it for hidden cameras and started unpacking.

What had I brought with me? You wonder. Oh,

this is fun, Detective. You see, Liam's father ran on a strict religious ticket. He talked about God and country. One of those guys. If he thought a church wasn't praying hard enough, he'd call them out on it, and God forbid someone in the church had a baby out of wedlock.

The VCR I'd purchased at a yard sale and the tapes, well, those were a little bit icky. I went to several adult shops over the last few months and picked up every type of fetish video I could find. I used a copy store's business office to print several pages of kinky sex instructions, articles like 'Bondage for Beginners,' 'Rope and Rigs', and finally, 'Autoerotic asphyxiation safety guide.'

I sprayed some of my wife's perfume around and laid out some women's clothing in his size, which I'd found at a yard sale, and lit some candles. His car pulled up, and I glanced through the window to see if it was him. The screen door opened, and I heard him moving into the trailer. "Someone sure smells good. How much time do we have?" he walked right past me, never noticing me in the closet. Opening the door, the music from the room covered any sound I was likely to make. I took the rope that I had hidden behind a drapery on the wall, placed it over his head, and yanked on the free end.

The rope was strung through several eye bolts in the ceiling; I remember something similar being used to load hay into the top of a neighbor's barn - with the right pully system, you can control a lot of weight with not much effort. So I had enough leverage to stop him from trying to escape as I continued to yank on the rope, pulling him. With the help of the pullies, he was quickly in the room, and within a minute, I had him on his tiptoes. Thrashing around and trying to grab the rope.

I was wearing leather work gloves to keep from getting any rope burns and twisted the rope around and around the bedpost, just out of his reach.

He choked out, "They know where I am."

I almost laughed but looked at him sternly, "Who? Who did you tell you were going to fuck? What was her name? That's right, Honey 69. Have you ever heard of a honeytrap? I must admit I was hoping you'd put up more of a fight. But all I want to do is talk. If you just stand there, you'll be able to breathe. If you keep fighting, you'll asphyxiate yourself."

He stopped and really looked at me. It took him a few minutes until he figured out who I was. "Hey, I'm sorry, man, it was the tire..." his voice was cut off as I pulled the rope up higher.

"This is a little game, Liam. You lie; you don't get to breathe. You tell the truth, and you'll make it out of here." I felt a shadow moving someplace in the room or perhaps in me. The shadow knew I was lying. Liam didn't.

I worked on him for two hours. I turned off his cell phone and undressed him. You should have heard him squeal when I pulled out the ball gag and the open-mouth gag. "Hey, I'm not into that stuff," he cried.

"Well, the papers will think you were."

I turned him around and around as he spun naked. I could see him getting dizzy and knew that his air was cut off. Then, grabbing the back of his neck, I said open. He did, and I shoved the gag in his mouth. Then withdrew it and then again shoved it in. Over and over. I did the same with the ball gag. I wanted them to look worn and well-used.

Detective, I don't know if you know of anyone of the age who needs one of those little blue pills, but I knew that this brand took about an hour to be ready, as in things popping up. Well, as he was gasping for breath, I put a couple in his mouth and held his nose until he'd swallowed them.

The next bit was more for the papers than his punishment, with the ball gag covering any sounds. I mean, after all, we were in the middle of nowhere, but just in case, I kept the gag in for a bit as I lubed up a couple of anal toys. He screamed through the gag as I used them on him, over and over, before I tossed them in the sink. As if he'd planned to wash them after a good session.

For his father, I lubed up a medium-sized anal plug, and well, you can guess. He almost lost consciousness a few times and faked it once, trying to grab me. The lack of air had made him slow, and I, while not in my prime, was strong enough to take care of him. The anal plug had a nice red jewel with a silver cross on the end of it. The lady at the store had said, "I sell a lot of these. Your wife will love it. Make her wear it to work, and she will think of you all day." I don't know if that would have been true, but Liam didn't look like he liked it.

I removed the gag from his mouth, careful not to let him bite me. "OK, Liam, we're almost done. I have all of this on film and will edit out my face, so tell me about the cover-up. I don't want to hear any excuses from you. I want to know who helped you cover up what you did."

Looking at me with tears running down his face, breathless, he told me everything I wanted to know. "You can relax now, Liam; just one last thing for you to do. Thirsty?" I held up a water bottle.

"Yes, please," he croaked, and I gave him water and then waited for nature and the pills I had given him earlier to take their course. I think he was under the impression that I'd drugged him to put him to sleep, and the look on his face as his cock started to get hard was funny, to say the least. He wore an odd expression of excitement and fear.

"Play!" I commanded, but he didn't understand. "Okay, let me spell it out for you. I'm going to blackmail you. I'm going to use pictures of this to blackmail you and your father into confessing to killing my family and him covering it up. I'm going to make sure that your father, the Sheriff, and you, that you all pay. Think of this as your version of the Clinton blue dress, and I want money for my loss." In front of him on the floor, I dropped a blue dress and smiled.

Perhaps he thought he was going to live, and perhaps the mention of money was the clincher, but he took to the task at hand (pardon the pun) and started playing with himself. He looked up at me. "Are you enjoying this? You fucking perve, are you? Is this what you wanted to see?"

There wasn't much for me to say. I was enjoying the situation, not as much as what he was doing right then, but I do see why he was popular with the ladies, and right when he started to cum I pulled the rope hard so that his feet were off of the ground, higher and higher until he was swinging, and just high enough so that he couldn't touch the floor. He sprayed everywhere as he swung and jerked.

When he was dead, I placed a stool sideways on the ground to his feet so they'd think he'd been engaged in autoerotic asphyxiation and had his feet on the stool and slipped.

Yes, I know the blue dress was just icing on the top of the cake: "Governor's Son, dead. Possible auto-erotic asphyxiation." and "Crime scene investigation photos leaked. Sheriff denies the leak came from his office." My favorite was "Blue Dresses and Politics. Is it a trend?"

I took photos of the room and him hanging there. After I was done cleaning up any trace of myself from the room, I placed a very crude tape in the VHS player and pressed play. I could hear the moaning as I left, playing on the television.

Now, your gears are spinning. You've heard of this event. Am I telling the truth, or was this just something I've made up...?

Maybe it was a town councilman or a senator's son. I figured this would give you a gift of a clue to track me down, which will be fun. I've had plenty of time to change the way I look. I have one of those faces, like Ted Bundy. I look different simply by combing my hair a little differently, pulling it back, or brushing it to the side. If you do track me down from this, then good on you, Detective. You're as worthy an opponent as I thought you'd be.

I have to go now, did you like my gift? The latest victim, as the papers said, though they missed the point of her video confession. I hadn't planned to spend so much time with her, but I really enjoyed watching her beg for forgiveness once she was tied up, and confessing her sins bound like that, saying how sorry she was to her husband. He was one of those television preachers, and her confessing about every man she'd slept with out of wedlock and the money they'd stolen from grieving families was quite a revelation. Who would have guessed that she was responsible for so much violence against women? She claimed that her charities helped women, but in reality, she provided special services to high-society men.

She came to my attention quite by accident; once I'd found her and put her on the list, I just had to find the time. There's never enough time, Detective.

6

PREPARING FOR WAR

Friday, May 14, 2010

It's no secret that I'm older than you, Detective. I am glad to say that I still look good for my age. I can get a smile from a young lady working at a fast-food place and from those ladies at strip clubs trying to pay for college just the same as I can from one of those greeters offering food to customers at the big box stores. Please don't think for a minute that I'm bragging. I'm just telling you a little more about myself. I once went out with a girl, but we soon figured out she wasn't into me and we became close friends and she told me, "My friend Jesse says you have those panty-dropper eyes."

"What?"

She laughed, "When you look at women, their

panties just drop. But mine, well they may have shifted a little, but not far enough."

Jesse was her best friend at the time. Last I heard, they were doing well and eventually got hitched after same-sex marriage became legal. Kelly would have loved to have gone to their wedding. I attended to represent my lost family, and they made such a cute couple. I don't believe I mentioned that they came and stayed with me for a little while after the accident.

Of course, I didn't want company, but it did help to have someone else in the house. I was just waiting for the trial that never came and hoping for some type of justice.

When they left, I loaded them up with as much furniture as they could cram into their rental truck and offered to sell them the house. After my cleaning phase, I was in the clear-it-all-out phase. I'm not sure what the stages of grief are or if that was normal, but I just wanted to get rid of everything and move to the farm with Sport.

After the non-trial of Liam, I called a realtor and made arrangements to donate and sell almost everything I owned. I put a camper top on the back of my pickup. Everything I packed was functional. The only frill things I took were my photo albums. Kelly had done one of those memory parties and learned how to put together nice memory albums. She had three. One for her and I to keep, and one for each of the children. Her plan had been to give our son his when he started college—something to remember home by.

The only thing Kelly and I didn't agree on was firearms. I grew up with the Sheriff as a second father and learned how to shoot at a very young age. Actually, the first thing I learned was how to make sure the gun was safe and how to keep it clean.

Before we had kids, I used to have a gun rack on the wall of my office and one in my truck, and yes, I had some loaded weapons and access to shells strategically placed around the house. Maybe I thought the zombie apocalypse was coming. Shortly after we brought our son home, Kelly came into the office, sat the baby monitor on my desk, kissed me, and said, "We have to do something about those." Keeping her mouth close to mine, she pointed. Kissed me again, that playful kiss that promised more, "Do I need to beg?"

"Mm, No, I will secure them." Then I pulled her onto my lap and kissed that place behind the ear she liked.

"You know you aren't playing fair getting me stirred up. I'm going to make you a deal. I will secure them, but when he's old enough, I will teach him."

"Fair enough, and some parts are out of commission, but others aren't..." She didn't get to finish that sentence. The baby monitor chirped up, and our son needed something. You know how that goes, don't you, Detective? How old is your youngest? Those monitors are wonderful, aren't they? I love how they have video now. You should get one with better encryption. It's dangerous with all the trolls out there.

I went to the basement and a door that only Kelly and I had the combination for until our son was sixteen, and went inside. It was a small functional room. Too small to be a bedroom but big enough to hold the gun safes and a table to clean them. My son got into reloading for a while, so his kit was there as well, his powder in another cabinet.

I didn't have an arsenal, just a few handguns and a couple of long guns for hunting, no AR-15s or anything like that. Don't get me wrong. I'd own one, but I always liked how beautiful a shotgun was with a wooden stock. I wasn't keen on those soulless metal things.

When I left, I had a wonderful idea and grabbed the reloading kit. My son had packed it up when he planned to go to college and told me, "I'll save this, Daddy until I get home. One day, I'll teach my son to reload."

He'd been such a long-term thinker. I was usually in the moment. If I was hot, I'd turn on the AC or dress in cooler clothes. He'd wake up in the morning and check the weather. He'd dress in layers, and as the day heated up, he'd peel them off and add them back on if the nights got cool.

He'd picked that up from Kelly. Such a good son. Dammit, where was I? That's it. I packed up and left the keys in the reality box so that the house could be sold. The realtor was going to deal with anything that was left in the house and subtract it from or add it to the money I'd get when it sold. We had a few antiques that were from Kelly's side of the family. I sent it all to her parents, along with some toys that were Sports.

I didn't think I had to hide after my encounter with Liam, but I did just that. I went to one of my rental properties overlooking a nice lake. No, not Camp Crystal Lake... Is that a real lake? That would be cool to just visit. I do enjoy good horror movies.

After a month, and no word on any of the websites or blogs, or newsgroups, etc., and nothing in the news except that the Governor had dropped out of the race to spend more time with his family, I figured it was time to check on the Sheriff.

Although he tried to keep his office and rank when the Governor dropped out of the race, some of Liam's covered-up issues became public. He'd raped a girl he'd met on a dating site. They'd met for a drink, and he'd raped her in his car. If I'd had any doubts about my righteousness, they all disappeared. I was the one who leaked this information. Liam had confessed all to try and save his life.

It was unfortunate that the Sheriff was a recluse in his personal life. I guess making political enemies comes with a price. I found a place down the road from his cabin. I was a few houses down on his way into town.

I'd left my truck and other supplies at a backup location and took a car that I leveraged, OK, that I'd stolen from the airport parking. It was fun, Detective. Cars built pre-90s were a lot easier to hot wire.

It wasn't hard, and I kept my gloves on while inside the car. DNA wasn't as big a thing then—not used as much, if you will—but the O.J. Trial had already happened, so I was planning to be careful and wipe the vehicle down with bleach when I was done.

Anyway, then the boring part started. I put on a minimum disguise. I'd already let my beard grow out and had started wearing a hat. I picked another one from a grocery store nearby. It read, 'I'd rather be fishing'. Taking a small cooler of beer and soda, I sat and waited on the cabin's porch.

It was nice and shady there, and if there had been more land, I think I would have considered buying it for Sport and me, well, once this was all over. It took me a couple of weeks to work it out, but the Sheriff was a creature of habit, like most of us.

On Tuesdays and Thursdays, he would go to the old fire station. Someone had purchased it and turned it into a dance hall and bar. Beer on tap, and they supplied the mixers. Just a nice little bar. Did I follow him? Oh no, it was easier than that. Every time he went by, I'd raise my beer up to him. I did the same for several other cars as well. In fact, I raised my glass to most vehicles.

I was just a retiree sitting on his porch, drinking the world away. That's what I wanted to appear like. While everyone saw me, no one did.

I had an idea that might work. The following Tuesday, about twenty minutes before the Sheriff was due to drive by, I raised the trunk of my car and put the spare tire beside it. I put the jack under the front tire and, using a screwdriver, let a lot of the air out.

I placed the jack under the car and gave it a few turns so that the car started to rise. I got it a little higher and then went into my act. I started trying to turn the lug nuts—well, I was pretending to. On that flat stretch, he could see from his lane several hundred yards away to my house, and I had to resist the smile when he pulled in.

Turning, I looked at him with the brim of my hat tilted down a little.

"Howdy, Nighbor!" I called.

"Need a little help, Ole..." I think I'd done my

disguise a little too well. He thought I was older, and that's why he'd stopped.

"Ha! Caught you. Trying to call me old. My name is Evert Mills, and it wasn't for this dam arthritis. I'd have this done already."

"Sorry, my Dad had arthritis. Miserable stuff. Need a hand, Evert?"

"Nah, I got it; just taking my time. Beer on the porch if you want one."

He didn't, but with the practiced ear of a cop, he started to get to know me. Well, he got to know Evert. I didn't think he recognized me. He was just getting to know the neighbors, and I was glad that I'd researched him.

He was a lonely widower, and me a lonely, retired man with arthritis; what a pair we turned out to be. We became fast friends. Following the little research I'd done, I'd mention things to see if he liked them, and he would bring up something else, and of course, I told him I loved to play gin rummy. To be honest with you, Detective, I sat in on a few games when my parents played, but wow, I couldn't tell you how to play for the life of me, so I studied up after he mentioned he'd come over to play.

When we'd finished, I turned on the outside hose and cleaned up a little. He had no desire to come into my house, and I was supposed to feel the same about his home. Back then, in the country, if you were lucky enough to get invited to the porch, you were on your way to being friends.

"I've got a cold one if you like Schlitz." And that was all it took. He sat on the porch for a little while, then asked me if I wanted to go to the firehall.

"No, I can't," I answered, "grandkid's supposed to call, and I don't have one of those cell phones yet. Too damn expensive on my pension. Tell you what, if you see me on the porch when you come back, stop. I'll see if I can figure out my satellite dish. I hear there's boxing any time of the day."

I knew he wasn't a boxing fan, and I'd said that on purpose. I didn't want him inside.

"Sunday's the 500; why don't you come by and watch the race," he suggested.

"Love to. That's your place over there? I recognize your car."

Oh, I must scoot, Detective. I have someone that I need to go visit now before he gets away. Do you know that sniveling little shit who's been printing up some of the phony information you leaked of me? Well, I wrote to him and told him if he didn't stop, I would... well, you'll see soon enough.

7
FIVE HUNDRED WAYS TO DIE ON A SUNDAY

MILNER DAILY

REPORTER'S BODY FOUND — MONDAY MAY 17, 2010 — PRICE $1.25

Reporter Latest Victim of Adonis

By Megan Anderson

Kent Green, a reporter for this newspaper, went missing last Friday and has not been seen or heard from since. Kent was a loud critic of the police and was investigating a tip regarding the "Adonis" serial killer, sent in to the paper's hotline.

Kent was looking into the serial killer's possible motivations and had called "Adonis'" mental capacity into question, while wondering if there might be a sexual motive for the killings.

Police has updated their suspect's sketch, based on the reports of witnesses at the alleged crime scenes. One witnessed stated that the alleged killer was wearing a baseball cap.

IS THIS THE ADONIS KILLER?

MONDAY, MAY 17, 2010

Hi Detective, did you get my gift? That sniveling little shit put up more of a fight than I would have thought possible, and at my age, well, that was no fun. Since you discovered me, I have stopped, as you've noticed, trying to hide those that I have crossed off my list. When I've completed it, I'll close up shop and move on, just like Santa.

I don't think I told you, but Sport and Kelly's

parents all passed. Died of natural causes, as they say. My plans for us retiring together are gone, but Sport had a wonderful life with Kelly's parents. The neighbors had young kids, and they all adopted him. I remember her Dad telling me, "Come visit, that crazy son of a... neighbor put in a dog door. Now Sport can come and go between our house and theirs anytime he wants; you should see him with the kids." Someone else must have entered the room, or he would not have curbed his language. I was glad that Sport found his place in this world.

They're all buried in the plots my mother-in-law had purchased. Only Kelly's parents knew this, but they'd made arrangements for me to plant a tree on one of their plots. While digging a hole, I placed Sports' body in it. I just wanted to keep the family together.

There's now nothing holding me back from moving on to a new life. I hear Rio is fun. I can picture myself now lying on the beach in Rio, relaxing in one of those thong bottoms.

OK, don't picture me like that, please. I may look good, and at one point, I thought about trying to be a bodybuilder. My wife said I had an obsessive gene, and once I start something, I must finish it. I was that way at the gym. What started as a three-day-a-week, just-get-out-of-the-house workout quickly turned into weeks where I'd do twice-daily workouts. I'd be up at the crack of dawn and then go all out again in my garage in the evenings.

I look back on that now as a time that I was away from my family. If I could get rid of all of that gym time to have a few hours more with my family, I would gladly do it. How is it for you? I've seen you jogging lately, working off the stress of your job, I guess. If it's because of me, I'm really sorry. I promise, in another three, maybe six months, I'll be done.

Will you have my name by then? Will you know who I am so that my passport becomes useless? Do you know about my other passports? Well, I have another gift for you, since I'm sure that the stress from your bosses is something that has affected your life. My life insurance policy needed updating, so I've left a will and named you and your family as the beneficiaries. I know you don't have to thank me. Think about it. Kill me, and you get a one-million-dollar payoff.

Yes, I did say, "kill me." Because what I'm doing is serving justice, and even though by the laws of this land, they would call me a murderer, a serial killer, a psychopath, I am really just a man looking for payback. Who knows, by doing this, I may keep some other mixed-up little kid from getting pissed on, and the people at the drive-through will really check to make sure that it's 'Ketchup only!' on the hamburger and no cheese. I know one snot-nosed pimple-faced boy at Circle King who'll never mix up a drive-thru order again after tonight. Nothing gets me more upset than getting hosed in the drive-thru. Last night, I called, pretending I wanted a job for my son, and asked what time the afterschool shift typically gets off. I'll be going there soon to see why he messed up my order, talk to him in the parking lot, and maybe introduce him to a new tool I have that I need to test out.

Shit, where was I? Oh, the Sheriff. My god, I'd underestimated him. But he'd also underestimated me. I arrived shortly after the race started. I could hear the engines from outside. He had the volume up, making sure the world knew he was a typical retired person.

I've never been a race fan, but I am a car guy, so I figured I'd let things get going and work out a way to overpower him. I had a sap in my pocket, one of the old ones that the police used to carry.

I thought it would be nice if he drank a bunch, and then I could just run his car and him into a tree or something. I really hadn't planned this one out as much, and that almost cost me my life and my mission. Getting out of my car, I took my leather gloves off and placed them on the seat casually in case he was watching. I tried to make sure that I touched this throw-away car as little as possible. As I mentioned earlier, DNA was just becoming something criminals feared. I was more worried about fingerprints.

At the door, he smiled. "Well, hell, boy, you're late. Get over there and get yourself beer and some chips and whatever else you want," he said while offering his hand.

His other hand pointed at the table, but what I hadn't noticed was the shiny object on it. As I instinctually shook his outstretched hand, he slammed his handcuffs on my wrist, it hurt like hell, and I heard a click. Using that as leverage, he pulled me around and slammed me against the wall. Before I knew it, he almost had the other cuff hooked behind my back.

"Do you think I'm stupid? I never forget a face. It did take me a bit to place yours, but I know it's you. Things about Liam make a little more sense now," he was gloating at his apparent victory.

Seriously, this overweight, red-blotchy face retired sheriff just cuffed one hand and was about to cuff the other. Luckily, I was strong, as I mentioned. I stomped on his foot and threw my head back into his face. Luck and his overconfidence, only handcuffing the casual drunk, was what saved me. As soon as the first cuff had gone on, he'd been smiling from ear to ear.

He applied more pressure to the cuffed hand he

was holding, and the pain was enormous. I'd never worn cuffs for real before.

He grunted, "We've got a fighter here; I'm going to take you in myself."

He pinned down both my arms, still trying to get them cuffed. I jumped up in the air, put my feet on the wall, and pushed away, which drove us both back and further into the living room. Luck was on my side because he tripped on a stand, and we both went down to the floor. I could hear the wind knocked out of him.

Still lying on top of him, I drove the back of my head into his face two or three times, maybe more. I sort of switched to reflexes in that instant. Add that to the fact that I was dizzy, and I may have lost a few seconds of consciousness before I turned over, straddling him, and used the cuffs as leverage to choke him. I pulled the cuffs around his fat neck as close together as I could.

I'll give the Sheriff his due. He started to fight back, and I felt his hands moving underneath mine. I remember Officer Conrad showing me that move. I'm not sure what it's called, but as soon as his hands started to move, I picked his head up and slammed it down on the hardwood floor again and again until he lost consciousness.

I searched him, found the keys for the cuffs, turned him over, and put them on him. I stood and looked around. Waited until I was sure there was no one else home. I wondered whether he'd called for backup before I got there, figuring he would catch me and make a big deal of the arrest. He could have seen easily enough when I'd left the cabin.

Looking down at him, I couldn't think of a good way to cover his wounds and make them appear natural. "You almost had me. I'll give you that, Sheriff," I said as I picked his unconscious body up in a fireman's carry. At the door, I looked around, but I didn't see anyone on the road. I placed him in the trunk and quickly tied his legs with some hay baling string. I didn't bother with his hands as he was cuffed, and this would keep his legs from moving too much.

I put on leather gloves, grabbed a towel and bleach, and ran into his cabin. I figured I didn't have much time, but I did my best to straighten the place up and wipe the blood off the floor. I cleaned more blood on the back of the sofa with the bleach.

It wasn't perfect, and if I'd made those attempts at hiding my traces today, the police would have figured it out immediately. But back then, I hoped to get a few hours head start. I hopped into my car and headed for the main road. It took me a second to work out where the police would most likely be coming from, and I turned in the opposite direction. Luckily, I'd picked the right direction. As I was going over a small hill, I could hear sirens and see lights behind me. I breathed a sigh of relief as they turned into his lane. I couldn't hear any sound from the trunk as we drove.

Can you imagine Detective? This officer almost stopped me after I had completed scratching just one of the people off the list. That would have driven me insane. I cursed myself as I drove all afternoon and then into the night. I figured my cabin was already being searched, so I just kept driving. A few hours into the trip, I heard him start to move around. I figured he was planning something for the moment when I'd open the trunk.

Whir sat beside me in the passenger seat, smiling, not saying a thing. I could tell that he was enjoying himself. I hadn't seen him in a while, but I always knew he would be back.

"I gave you your privacy with Liam."

"Thank you."

We lapsed into silence. It felt as though we were two weary co-workers with an unfinished task. As darkness fell, I pulled into a small campground. Judging by the signage and litter, it seemed frequented by scout groups and lovers. There was a scenic overlook that must have been popular during the fall. I hoped that we would have some privacy and that I could re-secure him. After, come up with some sort of plan. But really, it was not going as I wanted at all. "Nice area; I think this should work. I don't see anyone around," Whir said.

I tried to ignore him but knew his knack for detection surpassed mine, so I simply nodded. Ignoring him and hiding things from him wasn't my forte back then, but I've since improved.

I strongly suspected he knew the last person on my list, which undoubtedly troubled him. As we sat side by side, Whir suddenly shouted, "Look out!" just as a shot rang out, narrowly missing my face. I could almost hear the bullet's whistle as it hit the windshield. I watched the glass splinter in slow motion. If not for Whir's warning, the Sheriff, battered and bruised, might have been hailed a hero. It turned out the Sheriff not only had another handcuff key but also a gun, though I couldn't tell the caliber at the time. Nonetheless, there was now a hole in the windshield.

I jammed my foot all the way down and cut left and right as two more shots went wild. Then, the shooting stopped. I assumed he was waiting for a stable shot. That suggested he likely had a small revolver with limited ammunition, perhaps five or six shots.

With one or two more chances remaining, I sped down the road, my headlights showing only what lay immediately ahead. I saw the overlook, with a nice small stone wall. I realized I couldn't pull off any TV stunts where I'd jump the wall and send him down to his doom, so I drove straight at the wall, my seat belt on. The car was from the 90s, so there was no airbag to rely on. When I was about ten feet away, I pulled the wheel hard to the left and slammed on the brakes. The car slid sideways and slammed against the rock wall.

Luckily it kept running, so I kept the wheel turned to the left, and it limped the rest of the turn until I was going straight back the way I'd come. I heard him scream in pain, cussing me from the trunk. I stopped and jammed the car in reverse, and floored it again, this time going backward as fast as it would go. The car coughed and sputtered, and I heard the squeal of the engine as I crashed into the wall again.

We hit like a ton of bricks, and for a second, I lost consciousness. I placed it in drive again; the engine was good. But when I pulled forward, I could hear the wheels scraping against the metal of the fenders. I pulled as far as I thought it would go and, in reverse, slammed it again against the wall. I didn't hear anything from the trunk. I noticed Whir was no longer in the car, but he was waving at me from a picnic table, giving me the thumbs up.

This time, I didn't hit as hard, and I didn't lose consciousness. I pulled forward and saw the trunk had opened as a result of the impact. As I didn't hear anything, I took a chance, got out, and walked around to look in the trunk.

He had one shot left; at least, that's what I found when I looked at the pistol, a little five-shot revolver. But he was not in any shape to shoot anyone. I switched off the lights as the car stalled. I poured bleach around to wipe away any traces of what might have been my blood in the darkness. "I would have loved to talk to you more, Sheriff," I said to him, looking down at his mangled body. "I wonder what they'll think. 'Jealous husband'? You did have a few women you were seeing, or did you call them and tell them who you thought I was? That could be it as well, no matter."

I grabbed my go bag out of the backseat and set it on the ground, a short distance from the car. I thought about keeping his pistol, but I decided against it; why risk linking myself to him? I cleaned it and tossed it in the trunk. My spare gas can was in the trunk; it didn't exactly conform to the explosive stereotypes of popular fiction movies. I bet it hurt like hell rolling around, and some gas was already leaking into the trunk. I picked the can up with my gloves on and poured it over the Sheriff. He was still breathing but barely moved as the gas hit him.

I poured some on the hood and finally some on the towel I'd been using with the bleach. Not knowing whether there would be an explosion, I put my go bag over my shoulders so that it fit crosswise on my back.

I looked down at him and saw his eyes open. I was glad that he was awake.

"I wish I had more time, Sheriff, I really do."

I used my belt buckle to ignite the old-fashioned white-tip match and tossed it into the trunk on top of him. The gas ignited quickly, and I moved back as fast as my sore body would allow me toward the tree line and waited.

I thought that the gas tank would just explode and the car would go up quickly, but it didn't. You should have heard his glorious screams, Detective, the way he wailed and moaned for help. I just smiled, leaning back against a tree. I could picture my son's pain, how he yelled for them to help his sister and my wife. This wasn't the justice I'd planned, Detective, but this was justice.

"Serves you right..." I started to say as I went around the tree, and just then, the car, or what was left of it exploded. The blast wasn't as big as you'd think, but I've never been that close to a car that was on fire to tell if it was big or small. It knocked me to the ground, and when I was getting up, I heard Whir trying to stifle a laugh.

It was night and I doubted that anyone would see the fire behind the tree line. We were far enough out in the country. I picked up my go bag, checked the area I'd fallen down on for anything I might have dropped. Finding nothing, I hit one of the trails that would take me to the river, and once across, I knew there was a train track I could follow.

At the time, I wasn't sure whether the trains were running. I'd always wanted to hop on a train, but I never got the chance that trip. I found another way home.

Detective, I do hope you are enjoying these little tales of how I got started. The only person I've shared any of this with is Whir, and the more I learn about him, the more I fear he no longer has my best interests at heart.

Enjoy the three-day weekend. I'm going fishing, so you should be able to relax with your family. I am really sorry about taking time away from them. It would be easier if they weren't in your life. Then it could just be us.

8

VACATION DAY

Friday, July 2, 2010

Today's been a fun day, Detective. I was so glad to see your partner get the award. She deserves it. Putting up with you is tough enough, just kidding, but it was wonderful, and her speech was inspiring. I think she should go into politics. Has she ever thought about it?

I didn't stay long. I had to knock a few people off of my list. Oh, where have I been? Wow, I'd almost forgotten that it's been a month, no two since I last wrote. I really should have kept in touch, but where I was, the Internet was unreliable, and I had no way of knowing what was being monitored.

I needed to cross some bikers from my list. I wanted to have a weathered tanned look, so I could spend time riding to get that look, or I could go visit

Belize. So, Belize it was, and I spent eight days on a dock working on my tan. Feel free to add that to your description. When I got back, I needed to go undercover of sorts. That's what I told Whir. Whiro, you remember him, don't you? I believe that that's where he was from, or at least he was worshipped there by the Mayan civilization, around 1500 BC.

I wanted to get a better look at a statue I'd heard about, and seen a grainy photo of in a brochure. It was in one of the Mayan ruins. And wouldn't you know, it was Whiro. There's no doubt in my mind. I took a small plane, then a bus alongside some tourists to the mainland, and from there, a nice boat ride down the river. We saw some crocodiles, but since they were only about ten inches long, I didn't think that I was in danger.

I told people I was a widower taking the trip my wife and I had always wanted to do, which wasn't far from the truth, with the omission of Whir.

Our guide was beautiful and had a wonderful smile. For a moment, I thought of staying, of forgetting the last people on my list, but thankfully, I felt a familiar chill as Whir appeared. "She's pretty; I wonder if she's one of my descendants?" his voice mocking me, all the while knowing why I was there.

Ignoring his quips, I asked, "Were you born here?" really asking Whir, but the guide smiled at me and whispered, "No, I'm from Loyalton, a super small town in California, but I visited here last summer and I came back to make a little extra money and get some credits for my university course. I'm studying to be an archeologist."

Whir turned yet more pale than he normally was and walked over to his statue, "What can you tell me about this statue?"

"I'm not sure if it's him or not, but he looks like Whiro, a deity from Māori mythology. The only problem is that the Māori are in New Zealand."

Whir stood still, and the shadow that normally kept circling him also stopped moving while she continued, "Whiro was one of the sons of Ranginui (the sky father) and Papatūānuku (the earth mother) in Māori mythology, and often portrayed as the god of darkness, evil, and death."

"Wow, how do you know all of that?"

"Aah, school," she giggled, "I had a class on the Māori, and when I saw the statue here during a visit, well I just knew that it was him. Now my professor said it was a coincidence and that there was only so much they could do at the time with the stone tools they had. But I believe it's him."

We walked around the statue, and for the first time in a while, Detective, I could picture something other than just pain. There was an age difference between us, but it wasn't as bad as you might think. Later I found out that she'd been married, but it hadn't worked out. She'd decided a few years before that her current career was not what she wanted - thus the new career, after college that was.

I knew my mission would keep me from being closer to her, so I made a motion of please continue...

"When I saw the carving, I dedicated a few papers to him, never mentioning Belize or the Mayans. I didn't want to get any points deducted for not being able to prove my statements. My only explanation on how he got there, if he was real, was that he must have gone to New Zealand (Aotearoa) as he fled to the underworld after his parents, Papatūānuku and Ranginui, were separated."

When I must have looked like I did not know what she was saying, she smiled. "Papatūānuku 'Earth Mother' and Ranginui 'Sky Father.' Their separation was used to explain the creation of the world, and some considered Whiro to be the origin of evil. The funny historical quirk is that they also believed that evil was necessary for there to be a cosmic balance. It was Whiro who tried to prevent his brother, Tāne from giving the three baskets of knowledge to humanity."

Whiro had been unusually silent during all of this. I smiled at her asking. "Who won?"

"Tāne, in spite of Whiro's efforts he was able to bring knowledge and enlightenment to humanity, and now we have cell phones!" We both laughed at her joke. I looked at Whir and he was smiling. Evidently, he'd decided that my knowing this couldn't hurt him and he was impressed by our guide.

Our guide answered some questions for another traveler, and while we were alone, Whiro put his hand under his chin and said, "I like her. You should stay."

"You know that's not possible," I answered, wondering if he knew of my plans and was simply trying to distract me.

"Well then, give her this hypothesis to write a paper on. Tell her that you've been studying me, and that's why you came down. I know this to be true; I'm not stupid, Charlie."

He told me his own version, and I smiled, amazed at his directness. Some of the things lined up with what I knew, he finished with a wicked smile on his lips: "You can be easily replaced, Charlie; don't ever forget that."

The guide pulled herself away from a couple who wanted her to be their personal photographer. I told her the backstory about how I saw the picture and had always been interested in the Mayans. Whir stood behind her while I told his story.

"You know that the Maya civilization predates the Māori by several centuries. Perhaps a powerful Mayan deity like Itzamná, the creator god and lord of the heavens, came across the Pacific to share his knowledge and culture with the Māori, but to keep it a bit more down to earth; what if a survivor of the Maya, say a family, through generations, made the journey?"

Her eyes were beautiful, and I could tell that she had thought something similar. "Or perhaps the Mayans had already sent out emissaries to bring the rest of the world under their rule. I love how we think that people did not have boats until so much later, anyway let's say that this group traveled, and with no written history, any knowledge that was shared was purely verbal. They would also not know the language of the places they traveled through, so confusion would be easy. Ever played the telephone game? I wonder if as the generations continued on their travel. I wonder if the god, Itzamná, a god people connected to writing, science, and agriculture, could have been transformed into Whiro when they reached New Zealand?"

I could tell that Whir did not like me ad-libbing the telephone game into his story, "I believe I heard that Whiro gave Māori their language and farming techniques. Could this have been what happened? Could really have been the hero of the story about the three baskets?"

When I finished telling the story, I knew it to be true—or somewhat true anyway. I had to change it a little because she might have thought I was crazy if I mentioned Whiro being a real god, but it fits with all that I had found and some of those other gods I had mentioned.

Her voice was that of a professor. "Interesting, but there are several problems – distance being the first, the next is a lack of evidence. I know you are aware of the timeline issues as well, and that is not even mentioning the mythological inconsistencies."

Then she smiled at me. "My professor mentioned all of these and even capped it off with linguistic differences. This theory would have assumed that the person could speak the different languages and wouldn't simply be killed when they arrived at the Māori."

She got this conspiratorial look in her eyes, winked, and added, "Unless, of course... Whiro was a real god and could speak any language he needed to speak."

I laughed and smiled at her and never looked once at Whir, who was laughing as well, more at me than at her joke.

We had dinner when we got back to the hotel. Just a nice dinner with someone. It had been a long time, and other than you, Detective, she was the first person who wasn't a god I'd had a real conversation with in a long time. She gave me a name with an @ symbol in front, for her social media account to find her on. "Say Hi If you find any evidence of Whiro or if I happened to be in California."

You should have heard her laugh when I told her that I was not on social media. We downloaded that app together. She took control of my phone and sent herself a friend request. Her skin smelled like an ocean breeze, a sweet aroma that carried through the salty sea air as she leaned against me while adding her information to my phone. The restaurant's windows were open, and I could hear waves crashing and tropical music.

While this seemed like paradise, I knew that my list was not complete. I closed my eyes to take in her scent and the pleasure of her company and saw the familiar scene of blood raining down on us.

Later, I walked her to her door and kissed her. She was the first woman that I had kissed since Kelly had passed. I looked into her eyes and said, "I'm not ready for more yet, and maybe never will be, but thank you for this wonderful respite. If I die tomorrow, please know that I was happy tonight, Julie."

For that, I earned another deeper and longer good-night kiss.

Wow, Detective, that took as much out of me as some of the other letters I've sent you. You won't find the gang; they're not in your district. They're in Marston. If you reach out to the lead detective there, you'll learn about what happened to them. Blood did rain down. You should see the pictures. I pulled one of their motorcycles into the clubhouse and placed it on jack stands. I removed the faces of a few of them before they confessed. The blood raining from the ceiling was simply beautiful, and I swear I saw a rainbow caused by the streetlight through the window. A few of their wives/girlfriends were present, and, following Whir's suggestion, I had them dance naked in the raining blood. The police will find drugs in their systems. It took a bit, but I was able to make them all pay. The women weren't guilty of anything other than having chosen their men poorly. Besides suffering hangovers and coming down from the drugs I forced them to take, they all survived.

Ask the detective about the rape and murder of Jessica Hernandez. If the police search the clubhouse, they'll find her jewelry and some personal items from other victims in one of the trunks. Whir and I came across the gang, and I quickly added them to the list before taking my vacation.

Oh, crap, got to go; number 707 just pulled up. Isn't that a palindrome? The same numbers forward or backward? Whir is nodding his head, yes.

9
STALKING THE REPORTER

MILNER DAILY

Drive-Thru Mistake Costs Life | July 14, 2010 | PRICE $1.25

Drive-Thru Mistake Costs Life

By Jamie Atkinson

A young man was found dead in his apartment, the latest victim of the alleged 'Adonis' serial killer and what was this man's crime? What did he do that was against the so-called 'way'? I will tell you what he supposedly did. He got an order at the drive-thru wrong, and 'Adonis', this horrible man that some have called a savior, poured hot melted cheese on this young man who had only recently obtained his driver's license.

I've seen the pictures from the crime scene. The blisters and burns he suffered as he tried to claw himself free of the scalding hot cheese, that suffocated him slowly. I will never be able to forget the victim's terrified, hollowed-out eyes.

IS THIS THE ADONIS KILLER?

WEDNESDAY, JULY 14, 2010

That last letter took a lot out of me, Detective. I don't mean just telling you about my vacation, which, in some ways, felt like I was cheating on my family. But getting back into work mode after was tough. I'm not sure if you have the same problem, but after a good vacation, even a working vacation, getting back into the swing of things always seems to take time.

For number 707, did you like the gift that I got you from Belize? I know that it might cause you to have some extra paperwork to process. The basket was a genuine Mayan basket. I had an extra one that was a perfect fit for 707's head. Maybe I shouldn't have taken his head. But seeing him smile wearing that headset when I went back to the drive-thru made me think that there was nothing between his ears anyway. So why not remove his head? I enjoyed covering his head with melted cheese while he was still alive and screaming for mercy. I hope that this will send a message to all drive-thru workers in the future. "Don't fuck with people in the drive-thru." Please feel free to let the media know that next time, I'll have a talk with the manager and maybe add the rest of the employees to my list.

The basket, with its intricate design, took several days to make. The woman making it had delicate but strong hands. They are just beautiful, and I had no choice but to get you one. Hopefully, you can keep it out of evidence since my DNA's not on it. I promise. The lady put it in the bag for me.

Now, don't waste time looking at the airport security videos for someone carrying a couple of baskets. I had them in my suitcase. But you-do-you, as they say.

When we spoke, before I told you about my

wonderful vacation, I felt like I had to take a break as well.

After the Sheriff, I waited so that I would heal up a little, but also, I didn't want to alert M.S. Ellie A or the Governor.

I'm allowed to call her Ellie now. I asked when I introduced myself to her, but I'm getting ahead of myself. She'd moved on to a larger market, had a half-hour segment every night, and was on a weekend panel discussing politics.

As it turned out, during a follow-up interview with the Governor – Ellie managed to catch him off-guard with a question that echoed around the world, "Do you think that the blue dress your son was masturbating on had anything to do with your hatred of former President…"

The Governor got up and stomped out of the interview room, swearing at her. As she smiled and signed off. His microphone was still on, and everyone heard him shouting in the background, threatening her.

I admit, that made me laugh, and I considered sparing her, but if she had testified with what she'd seen that night or had made public the information I'd given to her. If she had just asked about a cover-up, I think things could have been different for her.

What, what was that… Sorry, Detective. Whir

just asked me a question. Well, more of a statement, he said, "Do you really think so, Charlie?"

He hasn't left my side since the vacation. I catch him some nights watching me sleep. Perhaps he's afraid that I will find out more about him. Maybe a way to stop him, but how does one stop a god? It would be nice to be able to talk to you in person about Whir.

The other day, I went to talk to a priest. He was no help, none at all. I could tell his mind really wasn't on the spiritual side. Especially seeing the way he looked at the boys. I don't know what they're called, the ones that light the candles.

What? Really? OK, thanks. Whir just told me they are called altar servers. They used to be called altar boys. I'm not sure if that's true, but this one was a young man, and the chicken hawk eyes told the whole story.

I'm sitting outside of his church right now, watching him take his nightly walk around the property. Whir wouldn't go in. It seems to me that he is afraid of the big 'G,' and he won't tell me why or even if God is real. I hope He is, and I hope that Kelly and my children are with Him, along with Sport. I may ask the priest about it later if, in fact, dogs go to heaven. Personally, I can't believe heaven would be wonderful without them.

Number, what number is he...? You might be

wondering, Detective, since he's the most recent on the list, his number would tell you how many there are in total. But some of the people I put on the list don't deserve the ultimate punishment. Some are just assholes, and I report them for their crimes, or I punish them a little, like your partner's brother. I slashed his tires. He was being such a shit to the waitress in the restaurant, and she did seem nice. Your partner's brother is not a nice man, but he didn't deserve punishment, well, at least not yet.

Anyway, he's number 723. Some numbers have been removed, and I don't reuse any of them. That would just make the notebook look messy. I simply put a question mark next to any that remains outstanding and move on. I do go back now and then and fill in blanks I may have left open.

Back to Ellie, she had moved and was very happy with a nice routine that was easy to follow. First, I knew where she would be each night, and as she was single, getting into her apartment was easy. Her condo was in an upscale apartment block. When I called to ask about a room and asked whether my dog would be allowed, I was quickly told that the only dogs allowed were service animals. Why ask about dogs? Well I wanted to make sure she did not have one that would start barking.

Ellie was a stickler for her workout program. She got up early and went jogging, followed by yoga.

After, she would have Jonathan give her a nice massage. If, for some reason, he was not free, Gwynne. A spark of a plan presented itself. I could wait at her condo, but I worried she might have been carrying some type of weapon or had decided to bring someone home. No, I had to be in control of the situation. If the Sheriff's fiasco had taught me anything, it was that I needed to plan more.

As it turned out, she had a favorite bar. Gables was its current name. I'd been told the original had been called Green Gables, but as it was, she liked Gables and would often sit and flirt with the different bartenders when Vince wasn't with her. Vince was her news director.

Steve and Stefan were her favorite bartenders. They would light her cigarettes and compliment her looks. Ellie was not a very deep person. Yes, that was when you could still smoke in a bar. Steve sometimes worked as the DJ, and Ellie would dance. Oh, how she loved to dance; most of the patrons had never read or watched the news, and she would cut loose. Taking her shoes off and just having fun.

When Vince was there, she would tip a waiter twenty dollars to get the big table in the corner where she could be alone with Vince. He was not a dancer, but he did love to watch her dance. Thinking back on it, I enjoyed it too. I started going on Thursday and Friday nights to get to know the people. I became a regular and always ordered vodka on the rocks with a slice of lime. I lied and told everyone my name was Dave, and "What up, Dave?" was how they greeted me.

Merrit was the kindest person on the staff. She was an amazing woman. When I drank too much or pretended to, she would warn me about the different women I was talking to with quick statements like, "Married, boyfriend, and trap." The last one surprised me; it was something that I wasn't familiar with. Later, when I asked, she told me, "She wants to have a baby, and you look like you could support someone with two or three baby daddies."

Thinking back, it would have been nice to stay there longer, but as it was, I had a job to do. If I had allowed myself to have friends back then, I would never have made it this far. Someone would have pointed out some mistake I would have invariably made.

Even so, I've had to change how I stalk and hunt numerous times. There are too many cameras around, and our DNA falls off of us all the time. But back then, combing your hair a different way made a difference. Add that to the fact that cell phone cameras didn't exist, and it worked out well.

Ellie would visit on Friday nights, sometimes alone... and she left alone or with Vince, as I mentioned before. After a couple of months of following

Vince and his family to see what his wife was doing, it was easy enough to figure out.

Vince's wife was sick. I don't know if they had an arrangement or not, but on Friday afternoons, he'd drive her to the hospital, and when they came back, she always looked like she'd been run through the mill, and when I saw the hair loss, I made some assumptions.

He would help her inside and then, after a few hours, would go. I assumed that after she was fed and in bed, he'd go out for a little fun. I never asked him whether his wife knew.

I knew that I had to stop procrastinating. I was enjoying the bar and the people, and they were my friends. I still miss them all. I waited at Vince's house after they'd left. I knew when they'd be back. He parked the car and helped his wife out. She seemed stronger, and under my breath, I said, "Good for you," as Vince helped her inside.

I waited a few minutes to be sure he wouldn't come back out and silently made my way to his car and sliced along the edge of two tires with my box cutter. Yes, he'd know that someone had slashed his tires and that Ellie was missing. But if tonight didn't work for Ellie and me, he'd see it as a random incident.

I had previously practiced on a couple of random tires to make sure that I knew how it felt. If you've never sliced a tire open, you won't believe how difficult it is. It's easy to snap the blade or have it bounce back and cut you.

The drive from Vince's house to Gables took very little time. I arrived before Ellie did and waved when I heard the "What up, Dave?" from Steve at the bar. Making a motion to take a drink with my empty hand, he nodded, and I knew he would have my drink ready when I finished in the restroom.

I pushed the door open and saw Stefan washing his hands. He looked up at me, and I joked, "Guess you all do wash your hands."

He smiled that wonderful, friendly smile of his, "Going to be a good night," and while he was talking about the club and the women, I knew that my intentions were directed at Ellie.

"Good Luck, I'll get your vodka ready," he said, heading out the door. I did not bother to correct him on the vodka. Two of them would be a wonderful way to start the evening.

Ellie arrived, tipped one of the bartenders twenty dollars, and made her way to the corner table. I was seated at the table opposite, looked up, and shot her a little friendly smile. There was very little chance that she recognized me with the poor lighting in the place and my hair the way I'd combed it, but I wasn't going to take any chances. The two drinks sat in front of me.

I started checking my watch about ten minutes before Vince was to arrive, made brief eye contact with Ellie, finished my first drink, and shrugged. When Merrit came to the table to see if I needed anything, I said, a little louder than I needed, "Guess she's not showing." As I ordered another drink, I motioned to Ellie as if saying, "Want one?"

She shook her head, no, some part of her was probably thinking this was a pick-up line.

"Boyfriend," Merrit said, and I smiled and said, "Thank you, darlin', always keeping me safe."

For the next half-hour, I checked my watch every five minutes, trying to be sly about it. Eventually, when I looked up, Ellie was checking hers at the same time. I smiled at her and raised my glass in a little salute, then downed it, motioning for Merrit that I needed another.

This time, when I motioned Ellie to see if she wanted a drink, she accepted, and to my surprise, she joined me. "I've seen you before, haven't I?"

"I'm sure you have. I come here all the time. Were you here yesterday? It was a blast. I work 2nd shift and have been using this place to get over my..." Pausing, I tried to give the impression that the drink had made me divulge more information than I'd planned.

How many drinks had I had by then? Well, The two from Steve and Stefan, plus Merrit, had served four more, but only one of the ones she brought were real drinks. The others had been water. Talking to the bartenders, I'd mentioned a month or so earlier that I needed to get in shape but that I loved hanging out and that if I drank water or something else non-alcoholic, people would think I was weird, so they started serving me water in a glass normally reserved for alcohol.

"Bullshit!" You say... Nope, I can still hear you thinking. I tipped the bartenders and Merrit very well, and they took care of me. If a customer wanted to pretend he was drinking, what did they care? I'd heard of bodybuilders doing this before, so I wasn't the originator of this idea. I just used it so that Ellie would have no idea.

My code word for Merrit on whether I wanted something with alcohol in it or not was the old joke, "Can you make it stronger?" Considering my drink was straight alcohol over ice, there wasn't much one could do to make it stronger. I made sure to mix in a real one every now and even asked Ellie if she wanted a taste.

A couple of girlfriends of hers came by the table, and she introduced me. "I work 2nd shift in Hagerstown." I said, "For the power company." I knew that there were multiple power companies in Hagerstown, for the city and for the county. That way, if I met someone who worked for them, I'd say, 'Oh, I work the other.' It wasn't the best cover, but dealing with people who had been drinking, I did not need to overcomplicate it.

Ellie danced with her friends, and I shied away, saying I could only do slow dances. A few songs later, a nice slow song came on. That was the first time Ellie kissed me. It was a good kiss, but my hatred of her made it a little awkward, and I almost lost her.

Not wanting to fuck things up, I made sure to finish the dance by pulling her to me, kissed her deeply, and ran my hand down the back of her neck. It was a move I'd seen Vince make, and he did know Ellie; to say she melted in my hands would be an understatement.

She gave me the perfect alibi, and I could've gone back to Gables after, but I never did. "Do you have a place?" she asked, followed by, "I can't be seen leaving with you. Tell me what you drive, and I'll meet you at the Ole Stone Restaurant... If you are OK to drive?"

I told her that I did and figured that whether she'd be there or not, at least this was an opportunity. As with the others, I figured out where I'd take her if I had the chance. I had rented several places, and once I'd used one, I would move to the next, only keeping that rented for a few weeks after. How easy it was back then—one could rent a room or an old farmhouse for a little bit of nothing and a handshake, whereas today, everything is on an app.

She did meet me at the restaurant. I was standing outside, leaning against my car. She smiled as she climbed out of her car, and her door had barely closed before she threw herself into my embrace. Her mouth was so alive, one hand around my neck and the other around my back. "I'm not hungry for food," she whispered, grinding herself against me.

We were parked around back, and other than the occasional drunk coming from the same bar we'd just left, people didn't disturb couples making out. They paid little or no attention. One guy interrupted us after I turned her and pressed her against the car door, pulling her hair so hard she moaned.

In a slurred voice, he said. "Got a smoke?"

Laughing, I tossed him the pack I carried to blend in, and neither of us paid him any attention. My hand moved down between her legs, feeling how wet she was. "Not here," I said, pulling back from her. I opened my driver's door, helped her in, and made sure I watched the show as she crawled across the seat.

"Like what you see?" she turned with that drunkenly sexy face that you and I know is not very attractive if the other person is sober. I used to go out with Kelly and watch people try to pick up and get picked up. This game would get sadder and sadder as the end of the night came along. We would watch these ugly people of different genders try to coax their dates outside before the million-watt lights came on.

Lost in my memories, I hadn't responded to her advances. Her bottom lip poked out, but that turned into a smile when I said, "More than you will ever know."

While I keep myself in shape, I've never been what you'd call a sex symbol, but trying to drive straight while she got undressed and then tried to undress me was a new experience. Kelly and I had never made out in a car until our son was old enough to babysit our daughter.

Laughing, we went for it like teenagers that night. Those memories put me in a foul mood as I felt Ellie A stroking my cock. When she moved her mouth down, I sort of lost it and slammed on the brakes. I'd expected it, but she hadn't and hit her head on the dash. I gasped, "Fucking deer. Are you okay, baby?"

The rest of the ride, I played the dutiful date, "As soon as we get to my place, I will check you out and make sure you're OK to see if we need to go to the hospital. If you're good, I promise, Ellie, I will ravage your body."

She laid her head on my lap and smiled, and I

pretended to absentmindedly pet her hair.

"You'll be my new Friday night, won't you? "she asked, looking up at me.

The rest of the ride went as you would expect. I turned into my cabin's lane and drove around back. I couldn't think of anyone that would have followed us, but I always tried to be safe.

"This place is adorable. Yours?"

"Moved in a few months ago. They relocated me from DC," I said as I made a big show of opening the door for her.

"My lady," I said, holding out my arm, and together we walked into the house. In the kitchen, she turned and started kissing me, pushing her tongue down my throat. With a move I was sure she'd practiced, she reached behind her back, and while we were kissing, her dress fell to the floor.

"Surprise," she moaned into my mouth while moving my hand between her legs, "I took them off in the bathroom and forgot to put them back on."

Everyone has urges. I have to be honest, Detective, I wanted this woman. I wanted to fuck her to death. Figuring that wasn't possible, I grabbed her arms so that I could get a look at her. I spun her around with a move I'd practiced and took the belt off of the refrigerator. I had it looped already when she'd had her back to me. I'm not sure what she thought, but once it was around her neck, I pulled hard as I kicked her in the back, just above her ass, which made her trip and fall forward.

I rode her down to the ground, just the way you see the rodeo people do on television, and pressed my knee into the small of her back as she flailed around. She grabbed for the belt, trying to turn over, but she wasn't able to get to anything on me to scratch me or to turn over.

She was a fighter, but the booze and smoking had zapped her endurance. It was interesting to watch her movements slow until she passed out.

I took her outside and waited for her to wake up. She was not out for too long when sounds of her sloshing around in the old chest-type freezer I had placed her in. The top was open and after a moment,

Her voice was weak and disoriented. "What? Where am I?"

I had turned the lights so she could not see where she was. I stood above her with a satisfied grin on my face. "Why, Ellie, didn't recognize me? Do you remember Liam? Or Sheriff Elder? My darling, your hands are covered in so much blood for what you have done, or should I say didn't do. Ellie, I've placed you in a time capsule of sorts. I'm going to give you exactly what you always wanted. You'll be famous. Everyone will be asking the same question. It will be the same question they ask in that children's book. You know the one. The boy on the cover in the striped red and white shirt. Instead of 'Waldo?', it will be, Where's Ellie A?"

I thought of my family and how she could have helped provide justice if she had only investigated, but instead, she went for career advancement.

Her scream brought me out of my memories, "Where am I? What is this? It's not water." When she asked that I turned on the flashlight and pointed the beam down into the hole in which I'd placed an old freezer, the lid currently up. At first, she couldn't see because of the light being in her eyes, but I could see her lying naked, in the blood, and Detective, I don't think I'd seen a woman as beautiful in a long time. Don't tell Kelly, but I thought of joining her down there in the blood. If it had been human blood, I may have, but it was pig's blood. Ellie didn't know that.

I moved the light to the side so that she would get the full effect; she was lying with her back against one of the sides, her knees pulled up to her chest. The bottom was covered in coagulated blood; seeing it, she started to thrash around, screaming and kicking. After that, she tried to stand up, but slipped each time and fell back down.

I waited, enjoying the show, and when she was finally to stand, I smacked her back down into the freezer. "Look at the beautiful blood on you, Ellie;

you haven't even asked whose it was, you heartless reporter."

She then turned over, and I swear, tried to seduce me, to beg me, even saying how we could have something special and go after the Governor Pratt together. I was tempted. I hate to admit it. But when she saw the smile on my face, she started screaming and tried to stand up again as I slammed the door down. I couldn't latch it at first. Her hand was between the side and the lid. I pulled up the lid and slammed it down again. All I heard was her faint screams as she tried to press herself up against the lid. The sound of her banging and screaming was one of the most beautiful melodies you would ever want to hear.

"Ellie, if you'd only told the truth. You had the platform to do that. For however long you have left in your pitiful life, just know that this is all your fault."

The screaming that had subsided as I was talking started up again after. She was whimpering and begging. I climbed down on top of the lid and hooked the chains around the top. For a moment, I thought about getting undressed and sleeping on top of the freezer, but I feared that I would want more from her. So I climbed up out of the hole. I could hear her pushing up against the lid, saying over and over, "I'll do anything."

The sound of the tractor covered her remaining offers and screams as I buried her in her living tomb.

When I rented the place, the owner asked, "Are you sure you can run one of those?"

"One of the first things my Dad taught me. I'll straighten out the driveway and give you a nice concrete pad area at the top, and maybe you can put up a basketball net for children to play on."

Detective, it was beautiful, and for a while, every time I heard a news broadcaster ask, "Where's Ellie?" I knew that she'd be happy. Why would she be happy? It's easy, Detective. She is famous, and that was the only thing she desired.

She is buried outside your jurisdiction, and now that I've almost completed my list, I'll let you know the address. She would love the thought of having one last news cycle.

Really? Fuck! Sorry, Detective. Whir just told me the priest is on his way for his last lap. I need to have a talk with him and I'm not sure he will live through it. Have I ever? No, are you sure? Wow, Whir is sure this will be our first priest; I think he's as excited about it as I am!

10

NOT EVERYONE IS PERFECT

MILNER DAILY

ADONIS KIDNAPS PRIEST — THURSDAY JULY 29, 2010 — PRICE $1.25

Priest Latest Victim of Adonis

By Mark Anderson

Father Holloway of Milner Parish, was kidnapped during his regular evening walk. The prime suspect is alleged serial killer 'Adonis' though it is not clear what Father Holloway might have done to incur the killer's wrath. According to anonymous sources, 'Adonis' has a reason for each one of his killings. The motive in this latest murder remains uncertain.

IS THIS THE ADONIS KILLER?

Thursday, July 29, 2010

Well, Detective, that didn't go as expected. Who would have known? Now, Detective, don't tell me that you knew we would make a mistake. Yes, Whir, even though you knew, you didn't tell me, and why was that, you wonder, Detective. Well, the great Whiro wanted to see if the big G would smite me or something.

Fuck, fuck. Tell me, Detective, is he alive? I read the paper, but I was worried about going to the hospital where I'd dropped him and his arm off. The cooler was all I had to put the arm in on ice. I hope they can re-attach it. Whir told me it's called replantation, and since we got him there so quickly, maybe there is a good chance they will be able to save his arm. I know, Whir, I do always try to make my cuts straight, but as mad as I was at the thought of him raping those... well, he'd looked at that boy lovingly.

Yes, Whir, I know, I know, I should've done a little more research. No, don't tell me that he's not like the boy in the drive-thru! That fucking asshole deserved it. What was it that the comedian used to say? - "You always get fucked in the drive-thru!" I bet those workers will think twice now when they check someone's order.

Fuck, how was I supposed to know that the priest had looked at the boy with loving eyes because he was his nephew? Should I have spotted the resemblance? Perhaps I should have, but things were just a little stressful. The vacation had taken so much out of me, and is my heart really in this now? Should I just close the journal permanently? I'm looking at it now, and the cover is quite beautiful, with the title "The Bloody List." Should I just stop? Dammit, Detective Lois, I never realized how bloody long the list would get.

Maybe I need to stop adding people to the list... Ha... But you're right, Whir. There are still people out there that need to be reminded of the path.

What's that? Well, maybe you're right. People and gods in this vehicle as well...

I just realized, Detective, that was the first time I ever used your first name. Is it OK? You're an amazing woman, and I'm glad you are with me on my journey.

Now for a more pleasant topic: I just loved the headlines, and I know the articles would have made Ellie smile. 'Ellie A, an amazing journalist, found! She was in her prime and will forever be frozen in time for us, her fans, and her colleagues.' A daytime talk show host said that she would have changed the world. That one was my favorite of all of them. You and I both know she was just a fame chaser, but according to the talking heads today, she was a rising star, and I'm nothing but evil.

'Who will stop this evil?' read another headline, and 'Could he be the longest-acting serial killer?' I don't think I am, but that's for you to let the world know, Detective.

'One-armed priest fights and gets away, screaming for help.' That headline couldn't have been more of a lie. Once I figured out... OK, Whir, once you told me, I applied pressure, drove him to the emergency room, and even carried him inside. Hell, they thanked me at the door.

I thought about staying around and taking credit for saving the priest so that people would know that I... that we were delivering punishment and would never kill anyone who didn't deserve it. Now I'll have to change my look again. It's funny. I think that by the time I'm done, I won't have any hair left.

Ha, yes, that is funny... Whir just said, "A one-armed priest walks into a bar would be the perfect start of a joke."

Oh, did you like the hat I had on? "Is That Fish I smell, Or Are you the one for me?" They are calling me the fisherman now. If they only knew that I've only fished a few times in my life. But I did find a deal for several of these hats a few years ago, and I'm not a wasteful person, Detective.

After the encounter with Ellie, I took some time off again. As I said, the governor had a rough go of it in the press and didn't win re-election, but I wanted to make sure that everyone who deserved it paid the price.

What? No, she doesn't want to hear about that. No... OK, Whir wanted me to let you know what the priest saw when I cut his arm off. The entire process didn't take very long, and there was so much glorious blood. I tied him to a saltire cross or Saint Andrew's cross if you prefer. It was something simple to make, and using the cat-o-nine tails, I flogged him for a while, demanding he atone for his sins. I had seen old priests do this on different shows over the years. To my surprise, he did, but nothing about the boy or boys. He confessed to every boring little thing he'd ever done. Almost everything had to do with wanting and desiring things, but no felonies.

He started by saying, "I've worshiped and prayed to lady luck, wanting it to give me a good hand in the casino. I took the Lord's name in vain when I lost, and I did imagine sleeping with one of my parishioner's wives. She was so beautiful, and she had such a beautiful family. I was weak and wished it was mine. I looked down at her and other attractive women's blouses when I gave them communion. Later, I even pictured what I would do with them."

Whir and I looked at each other, confused. "You're obviously not going hard enough. He's making this up," Whir stated. I agreed and took the Sawzall out of its case, placed it on his arm, and said, "What about the boys, the blonde one I saw with you."

Well, I didn't hear it over the saw, but evidently, he asked, "Who, my nephew?" The saw cut clean through his arm and wedged itself into the oak of the cross. Luckily for him, Whir heard and already knew, and having his answer on if the big "G" would smite me called out, and you know the rest.

No, Whir, she doesn't need to hear that. She won't believe it. Oh, she can, can't she? Whir wants you to ask the priest what he saw dancing in the blood. You see, the priest was talking to Whir, not to me when I sliced through his arm. Whir started dancing in his blood while I tried to stem its flow. "Tell him again," Whir said to the priest.

"What?" The priest asked Whir and responded louder. "He's my nephew."

There you have it, Detective; I included a picture of what Whir looked like dancing in the blood before we stopped and took the priest to the hospital. I'm not the best artist, but ask him. Ask him what he saw and then show him this picture. It'll be interesting. Part of me knows that Whir is real and that he was once a great god, but sometimes I also feel that he's just my imaginary friend.

Where was I? Yes, mistakes were made, Detective, and in the end, I'm sure I'll pay, so I had best hurry my tale along. I need to get everything out before one of your team members accidentally shoots me during my arrest. No, no, really, I wouldn't blame them. It's happened before.

Your partner killed an unarmed suspect. She's not on the list, don't worry, but you know as well as I do that she was guilty. You recognized the picture of the knife the suspect was found with. The knife was in his right hand, but the suspect was left-handed. Also, your partner stated that the suspect pulled the knife from his right pocket. Well, how come that pocket contained everything from his keys to his burner cell phone? The left pocket was empty.

Things just don't add up; the suspect was a punk and deserved it. He'd raped several women, and I'm not one to judge. I'm just saying that accidents happen, and I wouldn't hold it against you if something like that happened to me.

I hope that it doesn't happen like that. If you catch me, I don't know that you could kill me. You call me a serial killer, and in life, we never know what will happen. I do know that a lot of quote serial killers unquote thought they were smarter than the police, only to make a stupid mistake.

One of my mistakes was going after the priest. I also made mistakes when I went after the Governor. You see, he was the first person I went after who had his own security detail. Things could have gone better, but that is a story for another time.

Goodnight, Detective, number 412, is heading to work, and I must make sure that she still deserves death. You're right, Whir. Like Santa, we'll check our list twice from now on. No, that can't really be true. I know you told me before, but really? Detective, you may not believe this either, but Whir swears that he really knows Santa and was not lying to me when I was a kid.

11
GOVERNOR PRATT

Monday, August 2, 2010

The former Governor's home had been described by some as a stately chateau, and it was the pride of the town, brightening the landscape with its cheery limestone walls and the intricate carvings on the rails of the many balconies. The grounds were immaculately manicured, with lots of flowers and bushes. Even after his disgrace, he still had a lot of money, old money as they called it, and had turned himself into a kingmaker of sorts, forcing everyone to come and kiss his ring.

From his son's demise, he'd learned that security had to be top-notch. He never believed the stories about his son. Yes, he knew that his son had cheated on his wife and that his son's tastes were on the wild side. He also knew that his son wasn't a homosexual. You see, he had beaten that out of him at an early age.

"My son doesn't play with dolls," he'd yelled at his first wife. Later, he yelled at nannies and the different stepmothers he brought in to satisfy his own desires. One ex-employee even said that he was sure that the Governor paid one of the nannies to teach his son the right way to be a lover.

Detective, while the story I created about his son, with the video and leaked photographs, was something the public ate up, it didn't fool the Governor. I figured he knew his son was punished. I always read the newspapers back then and, more recently, news on the Internet, looking for anything that would let me find a chink in his armor or warn me of potential dangers. I devoured newspapers and information, making sure no one would me until I completed my list. While I was relaxing at a diner just down from his home on Route 11, I saw what could either be a chink in the armor or a trap.

'Security guards wanted.' To most people, this wouldn't have meant anything, but to me, the number stirred something in my memory. I asked Whir, who appeared immediately as I called him. I used to wonder if he was always there. I believe now that there is a psychic bond, and he simply knew when I needed him.

I asked Whir while ignoring someone looking at me. They must have assumed that I talked to myself, "Recognize the number?"

"Yes, that was Liam's work number," Whir said while stealing a piece of bacon from my plate. No one saw him. Unlike the priest the other day. That was still odd, and Whir believed it was because he was getting stronger. "Soon, I will no longer need you, Charlie."

Anyway, now that I'd established that I was right about the number, I went to the pay phone outside. Back then, they were on every corner.

"Hi, I'm Larry, and I saw the advertisement in the paper. Are you still hiring?"

"We need some people to start right away. Do you have any references and experience?" the lady who answered the phone asked.

"No, I'm sorry that I don't have any experience. I lost my job when the factory closed over in Milner, and everyone has moved on, but I used to be a bouncer," I lied.

"I know that closing was tough on everyone. Tell you what, come in for an interview. The Governor relies on his gut more than anything on paper, and if he likes you..."

"The Governor?" I asked, a little excited.

"Well, the former Governor, but everyone still

calls him the Governor, and someday he may be Governor again. He is working on a plan."

Back at my hotel, I pulled my hair straight back and used a bit of hair gel to slick it back. I cut the beard and trimmed it down to a goatee. I wanted to hide as much of my face as possible without shaving. I had never met the Governor, but he may have seen me or photos of me. I'd been quite vocal around the time his son had killed my family, but I'd been clean-shaven.

I borrowed a car without permission; well, I stole a car, switched out the plates, and drove up to the mansion. The sun streamed through the building's beautiful windows and illuminated the interior's smooth marble. The molding looked hand-carved, and if I felt guilty about anything, it was not taking my shoes off when I walked in.

The home had this old-world charm, and when I shook hands with the former Governor, I understood that this home, like his tailored suit, was simply his uniform. He wanted everyone who entered the mansion to think of him as an elder statesman.

But there was no joy in this house. While it was a cherished landmark that symbolized the close-knit spirit of the town, its insides were full of rotting boards and termites.

"Larry, it's nice to meet you. I may not need

anything or anyone extra. I'm playing things on the safe side," he said as he shook my hand. I noticed his grip was perfect, not too firm or too soft. He shook hands exactly as my real father had shown me.

'Do you practice shaking hands?' I almost said, but instead, I talked like someone desperate for a job. Which wasn't far off from the truth. At the time, Detective, the Governor, was the last person on my list that I really needed to take care of. Yes, there were others, but I could have retired after him and felt I had done my job. That's why I was just a little nervous.

"Don't be a nervous young man. My girl," he started, and I understood he was referring to the nice lady I talked to on the phone while belittling me the way his son had belittled people, "she told me you lost your job at the plant at Milner. Were you there when Jeremy was?"

The way he asked it so directly and with a single name, I knew it was a trap. "No sir," I answered, "I can't say I remember Jeremy, but I worked nights on the cleaning crew and doubled as security... I didn't tell her about that because all I did was tell a few drunks and couples not to park on the property to drink or have sex."

"Haha, lots of people used that place as a lover's lane. I even used it myself once or twice," he said.

143

Laughing, the former Governor patted me on the arm as if we'd been old friends.

The story? About the lover's lane, how did I know? Well, not only do I stalk people, Detective, but I watch them and listen to them. When I first started looking at the Governor in earnest, I spotted a man in the diner, Billy Clem, who was complaining about being off work, and the only experience he'd had was being a night watchman at the Milner plant, and Diane, the waitress, had said: "I know you were Billy, you chased me and old Tom off the property one night." They all laughed and gave me this wonderful backstory to use. I could have used Billy as a reference, but that would have been too easy to check.

"I don't want anyone in uniform. Do you have another suit?" he asked and continued as if I were just something he needed to decorate. "When you've filled in your paperwork, my staff will give you a slip you can take to Gary's Suits in town. He will take care of you. He does all my suits. Get four. That way, you can rotate."

The Governor went on to tell me that I'd be on the day shift from 7:00 A.M. to 7:00 P.M., a full twelve-hour shift, but since I had worked nights in the past, perhaps I would prefer working nights. "I want big bodies around me at all times. I know something happened to my Son, but I can't prove it.

That's why I look everyone that works for me in the eye."

I didn't ask about his Son. The way he'd made the statement, I was either expected to know already, or it wasn't my business.

"Oh, you have the job, but cut that hair and get that nut duster off your face. Clean-shaven is what all my people are."

"Yes, sir," I said, but I worried that he'd recognize me. Gary was nice and got me hooked up with a few new suits, all in the color and style the Governor liked his people to be in.

When I arrived back at the mansion, I met my supervisor and a few other people. "Easy gig, we just keep him alive. Guns aren't allowed. He has some in the house, but the only people carrying firearms are currently in law enforcement working part-time. He has connections, so we try to have someone on hand during the day and at night."

I asked about walkie-talkies or anything, and he handed me one that clipped to my belt along with something else I hadn't seen in a long time. A small metal baton. He smiled when he saw me looking at it and said, "That's an ASP, or expandable baton, similar to the side handle and the old Billy clubs, but this one expands when you flick your wrist, and you can knock the fuck out of anyone that needs it."

I had heard of an ASP, the surprised look was he

handed me a weapon I could use on my mission. I'd worked with the Sheriff when he first got them in his department.

I played it cool at first, just tried to get the lay of the land, as they say, and thought about the night shift. I did everything I could to stay out of the Governor's way, to keep him from recognizing me long enough to find the right time.

Most of his security was made up of ex-bouncers or police, "He just wants us to kick ass and drag troublemakers out back when done. He doesn't want police called or anything like that. This is the South, and if anyone is looking for trouble, it wouldn't be the first body buried on the property."

All of us in the break room laughed as the supervisor talked, and most of us realized that since the Governor was also the Son of a governor and a mayor before that, there could be many bodies buried out back.

My downfall occurred for several reasons - overconfidence being the most important among them. The supervisor called me in on my day off. By that time, I had a small apartment in town, and they had given me a pager.

I showed up in uniform, and the ASP and Radio were in the locker room, but they never let me get that far. I'm not totally sure who, but I think it was my manager who hit me over the back of the head with his ASP a couple of times, and as I lost consciousness, Whir said, "Oh, this will be fun."

If I'd been able to speak, I would have told him this wasn't how I would define fun, but that came later. When I woke up, I could tell that I wasn't in the main part of the house. I didn't make a sound, hoping that Whir was still around and would tell me what I needed to know, and he did.

"There were two of them, the supervisor Brian and Don. Brian is the one that hit you, and if your ribs are sore, that was Don's boot." Whir smiled while giving me his report.

Inside my head, I was screaming, "I don't need to know who did what then. I need to know what's going on now."

If Whir heard me, he didn't let on. He told me what I wanted, which I'd already figured out. "You're tied up with a couple of plastic cuffs. I think one of them called them zip-ties. It seems the shackles that are here haven't been used in a while and are rusted shut. Evidently, Charlie, you're not the first to be hung up in the old kitchen."

He knew I was curious about what he'd said and continued, "Don't you read history, Charlie? Kitchens in the olden days were little buildings away from the main house. Back then, the people in the main house did not cook for themselves if they had money, and also, because kitchen fires were a big thing, not like you could call the fire department. They went to get the Governor, and if you're wondering why your legs aren't tied, it was mentioned that the Governor would want to take your pants off personally, so he could cut off your fucking balls. His words, not mine."

I opened my eyes and looked around. Whir was, of course, right – there was no one in the room. I was hanging up by my arms. They must have bear-hugged me to lift me up onto the hook where the shackles went and then lowered me. My arms were sore but not completely useless. I knew the longer I stayed there, that would change. A few other zip-ties lay on the ground.

"The first one they used on you broke by itself," Whir said.

"Go out and let me know when they are coming."

"What's the magic word, Charlie?"

"Please, and I will owe you one," I responded, to which Whir pretended to be opening a notebook of his own and putting a mark in it.

The hook was fully enclosed, and there was no end that I could just pop off by trying to stand up or something, so they must have held me up, and one of them had zip-tied me. Looking at my wrists, I could make out three plastic ties around my wrists.

A small stool that must have been used to stand

on and apply the hook was in the corner, out of reach. It appeared to be oak or something sturdy. Whir, for as much power as he claimed to have, couldn't move physical objects.

I started to swing back and forth, pulled my legs back, and then pushed forward. Knowing I didn't have much time, I missed the first time, and my shoes only scuffed the ceiling. I started swinging again with more force and focus until I had a lot of momentum. Tucking my knees in and pulling up as if doing a core exercise placed my feet on the ceiling.

Using the leverage, I inched my feet forward as far as I could stretch and yanked. Nothing happened, except my wrists felt like I was slicing off my hands, so I pulled again. The next time, I gripped the hook and tried to dislodge it. That was what it needed and I heard it pop, and as it was covered in rust, it most likely wouldn't have held many more bodies up in the air after me anyway.

As I fell, I heard Whir say, "They just left the mansion." And since he'd literally walked through the door to tell me, I hoped they hadn't heard. I used the remainder of the hook, the screw part that was still attached to the cuffs, to twist it around and broke the plastic cuffs.

The only weapon I saw was the chair as I stood with my back to the wall, wondering how hurt my back and shoulders were. I landed hard, but adrenalin was on my side, I waited, feeling the weight of the chair, getting the best grip I could.

The Governor was the first in, opening the door wide and already talking shit to the spot where my body was supposed to be, "Kill my Son, I will make you...," he stopped mid-sentence.

He was already in the room with Brian, my supervisor. I pushed the door shut as hard as I could with my shoulder, and it hit Don in the face; I heard him scream in pain. He had started to rush in behind them. I brought the chair down on Brian's head. Remember, Detective, that Whir had told me that it had been Brian who'd hit me. I hit him twice more. I bent down quickly and grabbed his ASP. I did not have any time to rest; Don kicked the door in. The Governor understood right away that I'd freed myself and started to run as people do in comedy movies. He was just reaching for the door when it splintered open and slammed into his face, shattering his nose. There was blood flying everywhere.

Don, surprised and horrified by what he'd done, paused in his tracks, and that was all the time I needed. I pulled him into the kitchen and hit him several times in the face, head, and neck with the ASP. I hit him in all of the places that the original instructor said to "Not Hit" when they trained my father's deputies. Don collapsed and lay unconscious beside Brian.

The Governor started screaming, holding his nose. I wasn't sure whether he was screaming at me or in general frustration.

I pulled a knife out of Brian's sock. I'd seen it there when I first met him. The knife was not the cheap plastic kind with the whale on it that I'd had. This one was a nice, sharp lock blade that I swung and opened with one hand. I'd practiced this with other knives and figured Brian for the type to keep it oiled and loose. It felt good in my hand, and I thanked the unconscious man.

My moral dilemma popped up again - was security as guilty as the Governor? I thought about it, but then I surprised myself and slit both their throats, quickly and without comment, while the Governor watched. They'd attacked me, and that made them guilty.

"Mr. Governor, we meet again for the first time. I'm sure you know who I am, and now I'll get to know you."

Detective, I'm not ashamed to say that I enjoyed stripping him, and my knife, or my new knife or, more correctly, Brian's old one, was sharp. Hearing his screams was delicious. It didn't make up for him helping M.S. Ellie A to cover up my family's murder, but it did feel good to see him punished.

Other than a few deer, I'd never skinned anything, and the Governor was my first human, I took my time and tried to keep him alive and awake as long as possible. He died faster than I had wished, but he knew what was going to happen because I'd told him everything in great detail before I'd started.

The first bit I cut off him wasn't what you'd expect. I cut off his eyelids and sliced them as best I could so that he couldn't close his eyes to block anything out. Perhaps you've seen A Clockwork Orange, which came out in 1971 and starred Malcolm McDowell. There was a scene where they held his eyes open and then misted them so that they would not dry out. I didn't have any mist but I found water in the kitchen. It was such a satisfying moment, Detective. I could have retired then.

I'll tell you why I didn't, but that's getting ahead of myself. Number 230 is in my sights. Yes, I'm using a rifle this time; in fact, it was his rifle. He'd murdered his son, claiming that it was a hunting accident. I'll be back…

I'm sorry it took a little longer, Detective. I'm back. I had hunted a few times when younger with the Sheriff, and besides the company we kept while hunting, I didn't particularly enjoy the killing.

Sitting beside the Sherriff rifles, pointing in a safe direction, waiting for our prey. "My father taught me how." he'd said, "Charlie, I always wanted to be a police officer, and he thought it was important that I know what killing was. I think it gave me respect for the power to choose life and death over something, and I want that for you."

Anyway, the main thing we did each time was to put on our orange vests. The Sheriff took me out and had me sit in a specific spot and watch in a certain direction. "Don't shoot just anything. Make sure it's a deer, make sure it's a buck, and if you see orange, don't shoot." Anyone who hunts with their guardian knows this, and 230 knew it and should have seen his son, who wore his orange vest and orange camouflage pants, but his father claimed he didn't see him.

Yes, yes, accidents do happen, but earlier that year, he'd put extra life insurance on not only his wife but also his son. He'd told his wife it was just something his company was offering. I spoke to HR as if applying for one of their jobs, and they didn't list this as a benefit.

Number 230 killed his son for money. There was no choice really, he had to die. The first shot went into his left leg, then as he lay on the ground, the second shot maimed one of his arms, and finally, as I walked up to him, I told him, "This is for your Son," and shot him in the face.

My car was parked close to his house. I dropped the gun and drove away. I'm getting to the end of my list, detective. He had been on it for a while, ever since his wife had fallen down the stairs. By some miracle she survived, amazing, really. I had given him the benefit of the doubt when he'd shot his son, but he was too greedy, and when I spoke to his wife in the hospital, she told me she was afraid to go home. Well, now she'll be able to go home without worries.

    Yes, Whir, another satisfied customer.

12
MISSING

MILNER DAILY

OFFICER MISSING — WEDNESDAY AUGUST 18, 2010 — PRICE $1.25

Detective Martinez's partner missing

By Jeff Piatt

While the police have had the "Adonis" serial killer listed as their most wanted for some time, the story has taken another bizarre twist. Detective Martinez's partner, Shelly, has been kidnapped and is presumed dead.

An anonymous source inside the police department stated that the alleged killer's communications have turned increasingly frantic. All reserve officers have been asked to report for duty. The police commissioner is forming a new task force to try recover their missing officer.

IS THIS THE ADONIS KILLER?

WEDNESDAY, AUGUST 18, 2010

I just read the news, Lois. You have to know that I didn't do this. I'm sorry to email your personal email address, but with you being on administrative leave, I wasn't sure you'd be able to read your department email. Also, I'm sure you are going stir-crazy trying to find her. How are the kids holding up? Your youngest must be at the age that they'll know something is wrong but aren't sure what; just Mommy is sad.

The paper suggested that I'd decided you needed to pay for something you had done or said. That was absolute bullshit. Hell, Whir likes you better than he likes me. Always has, but we can talk more about that later. I found out a few more things about him and others that he talks to, but for now, we need to focus on your partner.

The police report said it seemed like she had pulled someone over for a traffic stop. Now, I know that she was more than just a patrol officer, and I didn't believe that she'd still be pulling people over.

I gather the police have already pulled the local security tapes. But they are still waiting for a warrant for the electronic ones. If you get me copies of those tapes, I can look for inconsistencies. I'm not sure that's the right word; I am so upset that I can't think straight, especially about the fact that someone would kidnap Shelly and then leave a note saying it was me. What type of monster does that?

A warrant isn't a problem for me I have already downloaded the cameras from some places in the area, including the doorbell cameras that I was able to hack into. The street over from where Shelly was taken has one of those speed trap cameras. I'm having a little trouble getting into that system; you may want to mention this camera to the detective in charge of the investigation.

If it's the person for the person that took her, I'm sure they would have been excited, and my guess is they took the first road that would take them to the Interstate, look for someone white-knuckling away You know, both hands on the steering wheel, squeezing. This person is obviously unhinged, so at this point, they might not even have believed that it worked. Shelly was obviously the target.

While the note was handwritten, the kidnapping was not a spur-of-the-moment decision. He, well, or she, but given the statistics, I'll go with him being male, had written it earlier and most likely drove by your home several times a day trying to work up the nerve.

I'm surprised he took her and not you. If I were him, I would have taken you, and that would have brought me closer to... well, myself, but you get the idea...

Sorry, I am back now; I spent some time reviewing the videos and saw several cars that could be of interest. Once I go through the footage again, I'll let you know whether there are any license plates worth checking out or whether any driver drove multiple vehicles down your street.

Again, that is what I would do and have done - rent a car with one of my many names and, after using it a few times, get another one. That was long before they had cameras in all the rental places.

Wait, damn, I'm stupid. I'll cross reference the cars driving by your house the last few days with rental cars and then hack into the car rental accounts to see what I find. You didn't know how good at computers I was, did you? We'll all of that I owe to Kelly.

She was very passionate about her work, and we would play this game called 'Capture the Flag.' Each of us set up a computer with as many security traps as we could think of, and then we tried to get past the other's defenses.

She usually won, OK, she always won, but the prize for losing was the same as the prize for winning, which consisted of hugs and kisses. Damn, I miss her, Detective. I miss her so fucking much, and I promise you if your partner is still alive, I will find her.

What? Sure... Thank you, Whir.

He's gone now, Detective. I am not sure what his last words meant, but he will help. "Charlie, I'm sorry that I ever doubted your loyalty to us, and I will check with the other gods like myself and a few of my protégés. I will always protect her, Charlie; you know that, and while you and I may be on each other's lists, she is to be protected."

Then he vanished. You know, Detective, it must

be nice to be able to instantly be wherever you want to be. I know he has a few plans left for me, and I can't believe he had anything to do with kidnapping Shelly... Is it kidnapping when it's an adult? Wow, I wish Whir was here. He knows these things.

I have to go. Keep your head up, Detective. I promise I will find her if she can be found, and if not, I will help you make the person who kidnapped her pay.

13
A PARTNER'S LOVE

SATURDAY, AUGUST 28, 2010

I could feel the pain in your soul during the interview, Detective. I'm glad they let you talk and ask the perpetrator to return your partner, Shelly. I hope it's OK that I call her by her first name. When I grew up, you didn't just call someone by their name until they told you, "Call me Charlie." That's why I call you Detective. Perhaps, in the event that we meet, I'll be able to call you by your real name, but that's for later.

A neighbor's camera pointing at the house across the road caught something. Most of the video was of the neighbor's yard, but since he couldn't place it facing the house directly, there is a side view of some of the road.

I'll attach the clips to this email. It looks like the

same person drove around the cul-de-sac several times over the last two weeks. Notice how each time he looked at all the properties except your house. He looked straight ahead, and the whites of his knuckles could almost be seen before he turned around.

In one of the clips, from a different neighbor's Ring camera, I saw one of those Door-Dash people pulling into the cul-de-sac and that time, he took the turn very wide. The camera caught part of the license plate, which I tracked down to Harmony Rentals, a small car rental place off Sunrise Valley. 'Car Sales-n-Rentals r-Us.'

I've attached a photograph taken there. From what I could find out, he rented three different cars. The last one matches the one that I found on the speed camera.

Shelly wasn't in the front seat. On First Avenue, a bank's camera caught the closed trunk, and part of Shelly's jacket—the one you said she was wearing—was visible. Check that picture out. I labeled the image-24.jpg.

I know. I have my own list to work on so that I can retire, Detective, but this is something I have to investigate. My apologies if I gave the impression that I was done. Perhaps Whir knew this was going to happen. He swears to me that while he knew something was going to happen to my family, he didn't know what.

"If I'd known your brother was going to die, Charlie, I would have told him to be extra careful that day. But then I..." he stops every time, Detective. Like he wants to tell me what happened to my brother but can't. Someday, we'll talk more.

As for Shelly, it's taking more time than I usually risk to find her. This isn't the longest I've ever spent in the same location, but I can't move. If I move, your people may find me by mistake. I have the computers set up and am using facial recognition software running in my lab. Kelly would have been proud of me. Some of it's open source, some paid, and I also have access to a couple of law enforcement databases, hopeful we can find the person that kidnapped Shelly.

You should check the juvenile records and see if there is any way you can find a match or anyone in children's services who recognizes him. I'm sure he has been in the system, and I bet that he has a long history of stepping up the violence. Unlike me, he wasn't rescued by a man like the Sheriff. Perhaps he started with animals, moved up to bullying people, and eventually to killing them. Shelly may be his first victim. That would make sense, while the timing, just after M.S. Ellie A's reappearance may not be a coincidence. I think he wants to take credit for all of my work, but that only works if he isn't caught. If he gets caught, they will know that he's only twenty-five years old, according to the driver's license he used to rent the cars.

I'm staking out a small property just outside of Stephens City that used to be a dairy farm when I was a kid, but the cows are gone, and all I see are lots of Christmas trees. Would you have trusted me enough to go on a stakeout with me? I know the answer, and I wish it wasn't so. You know how much I will miss you when I retire, Detective.

Killing number 230 was more fun than I thought it would. Sorry, I'm waiting for Whir to get back. He's taking a look around the property to see if anyone's hanging around the perimeter. I didn't want the FBI or local law enforcement to show up while I was inside.

Before I shot him in the face, he confessed. I told him, "I won't kill you if you confess into this tape recorder." And he fell for it and yelled, "I did it. I'm sorry I killed them both."

"Your wife is alive," I countered. That was the last thing he ever heard.

I left the tape beside his body, and yes, I'm under no illusions that people will claim he would have confessed to anything to stay alive, and perhaps he would have, but either way, I knew he'd done the deeds, and I know what I did was right.

Whir is back, OK? Really, you are sure. Perfect.

Detective, I've set this email to send in an hour. That should give me time to investigate and not be arrested. I love that feature. I can be someplace, and the email goes out at a later time. I never thought about doing this before, but I overheard someone in a diner. They used it to send future emails to their daughter for her birthday. What a sweet and wonderful thing to do.

Not to get your hopes up, Detective, but Whir said, "Shelly is alive, and while she appears to be dirty and bruised from the car ride, she seems okay. There are fresh fast-food boxes and a drink holder in the car, so he may be planning to feed her.... That or he's just hungry; remember how hungry you were after number 50."

Well, number 50 is a story for another time. But at least I think he's trying to keep her alive.

If I don't make it back, Detective Whir said he would come to you and talk to you. It's nice of him; after all, he was my only friend... before you, that is.

14
FIREFIGHT

Sunday, August 29, 2010

Detective, I hope they allowed you to get Shelly. I couldn't stay and wait to see if you did. Perhaps my disguise would have worked, but with me telling you so much about myself and the way I work, you most likely have a picture in your mind if not from the rental car company.

I was wearing the fishing theme, but I'm not sure which one exactly. It may have been my go-to 'No Bait, Try My Worm!'

Whir took the lead after we exited the car; he didn't have to worry about being quiet. I grabbed the Sheriff's revolver, not the one of the assholes who'd covered up my family's death, but my true father's gun.

"She's in the barn," Whir whispered and

pointed. I crouched down, hoping I had enough time. I didn't just want to charge in. I should have and maybe could have, but I needed to be smarter than this guy, and thankfully I was.

Whir didn't see them, and of course, didn't set them off, but as I was making my way 'low and slow,' as I'd heard that saying in a war movie once, I saw a wire. I didn't bother to trace it to its source on either end. I placed my hand on the other side and made sure that the wire was the only obstacle. I felt solid ground on the other side and made my way across the wire; I took a stick and placed it on the ground as a sort of flag to remind me where the wire was and kept moving forward.

It was then that I heard Ben, her abductor, ask several questions jumbled together: "What email address is Adonis writing to, and what's his email address? Can she contact him? Give me his email address."

"What?" she and Whir said at the same time I was thinking it. Whir continued, "He wants your email address, Charlie; next, he'll want to be Instagram friends with you." I think Whir was just showing off the modern words he knew more than knowing anything about social media.

Ben paced back and forth, and it occurred to me that he was a little younger than I thought, but he still fit the mental profile I had of him.

"Whir, watch out for the wires for me." Looking forward, I picked up my pace. I needed to move faster. Whir was in front of me, floating, seriously floating, while lying on his belly, his fingers touching the grass. He looked like a deranged Superman flying low.

There was a pole barn with a hay loft to one side. The loft had collapsed years before, and the barn's wood had aged to a perfect dark gray.

"Careful!" was all Whir had to say, and I slowed, looking around. The next trap was more creative. I could see several small holes ahead. If I'd stepped into it, I would have twisted my ankle and been cut by punji sticks. I'd never used these, but as I remembered, they were used as a booby trap in the past, the spikes driven into the ground at an angle to prevent someone from pulling their leg out. I wonder if he soaked these in shit or something as vile to later cause infection.

I avoided the last line of defense he had. Arriving beside the barn, standing with my back to the wall, not leaning on it because the structure might have collapsed.

"What's the email?" I heard him demand and then a smack. He'd slapped her. The thought of shooting him right then came to me when Whir said, "Right hand." The man had a pistol of his own, and right then, it was pointed at Shelly.

"Fuck!" Whir exclaimed, and I almost laughed. He didn't curse much, and I figured if I ever heard him cuss, there'd have to be a good reason.

"Show yourself to him," I mouthed.

He understood perfectly, "Worth a shot."

I watched the guy through a crack in the barn wall, hoping that he wouldn't look through it at me, so I kept ready to shoot him.

Walking to the other side of the barn, making sure he could be seen and that the man would look at him and not in my direction, Whir turned, smiled, and said, "Greetings, mortals! I am the great and powerful Whiro, and I have come to this modern age from the ancient days before days. I am the lord of death. I am here to bring my wisdom and power to your world.

I'm not like your other gods. I'm not stodgy or old-fashioned and watchful. I'm here to shake things up, and anyone following me will make those who are not on the true path pay.

Tell me, mortal, are you worthy of my new age of enlightenment? I am Whiro and all-powerful."

At first, nothing happened. Then Ben, at least that is what I am calling him as that was his name on the rental car form, asked again, "What's her email?"

Shelly's face turned in Whir's direction as if she'd seen or heard something. She was hanging by her arms. He'd ripped off her shirt, exposing her sports bra. Good pull, Detective. I hadn't realized how much of a hottie Shelly is.

Looking directly at Whir, her eyes a little dim, she asked, clear as day, "Who is that?"

Ben turned and looked toward Whiro. That was all I needed. I took aim and pulled the trigger, and my shot was true, Detective. Not a killing shot, but enough to make his right arm useless. It took all I had to not fire the second shot into center mass, as they teach. I could have killed. He has to pay, and simply killing him would not be good enough.

Arm useless, Ben turned and tried to raise the gun, which had fallen at his feet. His blue eyes were that of a man in shock. "Who, what?"

"Where?" I said and laughed and then launched into Whir's speech. "I'm an agent for the great and powerful Whiro. He has come to this modern age from the ancient days before days. The lord of death, he is, and he is here to bring his wisdom and power to our world."

Whir looked at me with an odd expression. I thought to him *Too good a speech to not re-use.*

"He is not like your other gods. He's not stodgy or old-fashioned and watchful. He's here to shake things up, and anyone following him will make those deserving pay. Tell me, mortal, are you worthy of his new age of enlightenment? He's Whiro and all-powerful."

I don't think I made Whir this proud of me since the day I'd set up Johnny. His chest popped out, and he stood to his full height, something he rarely did. Even I had to look up. Out of the corner of my eye, I noticed Shelly looking up as well.

"She can see me, Charlie."

"Yes, go to her and let her know it's OK and that the Detective is on the way," I said as a blood-curdling scream started, which soon turned into a baby's sob.

It was Ben, "It's not fair, not fair. You were retiring. Why did you come back? I wanted power. I would have shown them true power. You're nothing; you're pathetic. I am a better servant of Whir than you."

"Whiro's his name, and you aren't fit to clean his cat's litterbox," I said, stepping beside him and placing the gun against his forehead. He was leaking a little bit of piss down his leg, which mixed with the blood pooling on the ground from his arm.

"You know, Ben, if that's your name, you survived so far, and who knows, maybe they could repair your arm, and you would have lived. There would be a lengthy trial, and someone would claim that you were insane, but alas."

The second shot rang out loud in the barn. I saw

Shelly wince. Both she and Whir looked at me and then at Ben, who held his useless arm up to his ear. I don't know if he will hear well out of that ear again.

I shrugged, "I missed."

Whiro smiled at me, and he knew the real reason. Ben wasn't on my list. If he was on anyone's list, it was yours. But please don't get me wrong. If he were to escape and become a danger to society, I'd be back. But I understand that you want to make him pay your way by using the law.

That's one of the things that makes me proud of you. No, Detective, I'm not your father, nor am I even related to you. But while researching you, I saw that you were a hunter, and found we were a lot alike, and maybe I do fixate on you, or maybe it was Whir making sure that I was here in this exact spot to make Ben pay.

"What are you?" Shelly asked. I saw Whir whisper something to her, but I could not hear it and couldn't tell whether she had heard him. Looking up at me, she had an exhausted look on her face as she studied mine. Her curiosity having been satisfied, she smiled and passed out.

Leaving her tied, I picked up Ben and sat him on an old bench made of the same wood as the barn. I didn't figure that the rusty nails would hurt him any. I cut the sleeves off his shirt and tied the wound so he'd stop bleeding, then lowered Shelly to the ground. After I found the handcuff keys in his pocket, I uncuffed her and sat her on the bench. Then I hung him up.

"Please take me with you. I could help you," he pleaded.

"Oh really, do you see him?" I asked.

"Who?" was his initial response, and then he said, "Yes, I see. Whiro, he's right over there." Whir, as always, wanted to make me smile, so he walked to the opposite side to where Ben was looking and said, "Dam, Charlie, he's right."

Laughing, I thanked Whir and added, "Whiro, I know how to kill you…" Then, after a beat, I said, "But I won't. You may not be the perfect friend, but you are mine. Thank you for today, Whiro. Seriously, thank you."

Whir disappeared, Detective, he just vanished. I carried Shelly to what was left of the house, making sure that there were no booby traps around. The house was as run down as the farm, but it had a nice wrap-around porch and one of those sliding rockers. I left Shelly resting there and went back into the barn.

I didn't kill Ben, but I did strip him. He cried and cried when I took out my knife to clean my fingernails. I told him, "You're on my list, Ben."

I used his clothes to mark the traps, I called the police with his cell phone, letting them know that

Shelly was alright and telling them about the traps. I think I saw her talking to Whir as I drove away. I was sure he'd let me know if she was in danger until you showed up.

Detective, do you know how Santa is supposed to check his list twice? Well, that's what I'll be doing for a while. I won't be surprised if Shelly gives a thorough description of me, and I don't blame her. Things changed that day in the barn for me, not just between Whir and me, but things changed in general.

Do I have regrets, or as the tattoos say, "No regerts"? Those misspelled tattoos always make me laugh. I think between that and parkour failure. I could waste hours looking at those videos. But other than the priest, I have no regrets, Detective. I served my purpose, and if Whir is right, someone will soon take my place.

He never told me if he would start with a young kid who needed a friend like me or if he'd start with someone older.

I asked him one time if God, you know, the big G, was real since Whir was real, and other gods that I met seemed real. He quoted the King James bible to me, psalm 82: "God presides in the divine council; he holds court among the gods: 'How long will you judge unjustly and show partiality to the wicked? Give justice to the weak and the orphan; uphold the rights of the oppressed and the destitute. Rescue the weak and the needy; deliver them from the hand of the wicked.'"

"What's the divine council, and are you on it, Whir?"

"Bunch of stuck-up bastards." Laughed at his own joke, "You know, Charlie, I had a renaissance during the age of Solomon. 1 Kings 11:25-32: 'Solomon loved many foreign women, including women from Moab, Ammon, Edom, Sidon, and Hittite. These women led Solomon to worship their gods, and he built altars for them on the hills of Jerusalem. He built altars for Baal and Asherah, the gods of Moab, Ammon, and Sidon. He also built altars for all the gods of the foreigners who lived in his land, and he burned sacrifices in front of them. So, he aroused the anger of the Lord, the God of his ancestors...' So yes, Charlie, the big G is real, but as to why he gave you humans free will, that will never know, and promise you I will not do that."

I have a lot to ponder, Detective, and I'll write again someday, perhaps when I retire and get a rescue dog—a dog that can look after me. Enjoy your time with Shelly and your family.

15
DEATH OF A MOTHER

Monday, October 18, 2010

Detective, I am so glad that you and Shelly are taking time off. I hadn't planned on writing to you for some time, but further revelations about my past have surfaced, and I need a friend to share them with.

I checked on the priest again and heard from his physical therapist that his recovery is going as well as can be expected, and while I imagine he's in constant pain, he's making remarkable progress. I guess he can thank the big G for that and perhaps me for taking him to the hospital as quickly as I had.

In the old days, I used to search out stores that would sell newspapers, or I'd special-order newspapers from around the country, the bigger cities, and from around the world, but now I simply have alerts set up on my phone. I receive an email when someone's name or some interesting news from a town I've visited in the past shows up.

Yes, I have one for Loyalton, CA. Do you remember where the guide from Belize was from? It's my dream to move there, and who knows? The weather seems perfect there. Anyway, one of the online news sites ran an obituary from my hometown.

"It's a trap," Whir said as we stared at it.

He had appeared out of nowhere, "Where have you been?"

"Away, but this has to be a trap. They know who you are. You've given the detective enough clues. Any fool would know who you are, and she is no fool, Charlie."

"True, but I have to go, maybe not to the funeral but to the house. She's dead, and he is now a widower, I should go back."

"No, You should not!" It was the first time that Whir had yelled at me or yelled over anything that I can remember. I looked at him, my eyes full of love and devotion to this childhood friend, and said, "Just like with the attic. I have to go, Whiro, and you know it, the only question is, will you be brave and go back with me? I could never have visited the attic without you, and now I need you more than ever."

We discussed the situation in more depth, but I knew that he'd go with me. The family night and funeral were outside your jurisdiction, so the odds that you'd be there were slim. Still, if you and Shelly decided to make the road trip, she'd definitely recognize me.

Like hundreds of other funeral homes around the country, Jones Funeral Home in Stephens City was a long, multiple-room facility for visiting the departed.

I was early for family night and carried a funeral wreath with her name on it. I was wearing one of my many uniforms.

"Yes, through here, young man," the funeral director said, "I'm Ross, and she's through here."

I was quite surprised that he walked me into the room I'd been heading for. Believe it or not, I've not spent a lot of time in funeral homes. I did spend some time with number 119, a man with a dark side and a fear of being burned alive in the cremation chamber. I'd been explaining all his sins to him while I'd placed him in the oven.

"Please, no! Kill me now, but not in there; please, not in there. Not in there!."

I smiled a comforting smile at him, ignoring the puddle by his shoes after he'd defecated. "Hopefully, this helps you overcome your fear."

Anyway, there she was and I turned toward Ross

and asked, "Is it okay if I sit for a bit with her? I went to school with her Son, and she's always been nice to me,"

"Oh, you mean?" he started as I interrupted, not wanting to have him figure out who I was.

I shook my head and said, "No, her first Son. My mom couldn't make it, and when I told her who I was delivering flowers to, she asked me to pay my respects. She's in the nursing home on 11 and doesn't realize that people wearing florist delivery driver uniforms don't attend the family nights." I wasn't sure he believed me, but I needed a reason to be there that would not attract attention from anyone, and it was not like we had a big family.

"It's OK, Son. Stay as long as you like."

After he'd left, Whir appeared. "Son? Well, he's old; I bet there aren't very many people that he can't call Son or young man. Think you will live as long as the funeral director, Charlie?"

Sitting in the front row, looking at the closed casket, I whispered jokingly, "I assume I'll live until you add me back to your list, my friend."

"That you might, but who said I took you off it, Charlie? Now, want me to keep watch so you can say goodbye?"

"Please, and thank you, Whiro."

Standing up had to be one of the hardest things

I'd done in a long time. So many emotions went through my head. Someone had displayed photos of myself and my brother that she'd never told me about. He looked happy in them,

I didn't want to hang around too long just in case law enforcement showed up. I lifted the lid of the casket, and there she was, looking much like I remembered her. "I'm sorry, Mamma, I wish we could have been closer and that you hadn't thought of me as a replacement boy."

"She didn't think of you as a replacement Son." I almost jumped out of my socks, as they say, Detective. I thought I was alone, and Whir was keeping watch, but I hadn't heard the voice behind me since Kelly had died.

Turning to look at him, I said, "Why didn't you tell me I had a brother? Look at these pictures of you all together. That's not me." I was trying to keep my voice down, but the fire in me wanted to scream at him; somehow, I managed to keep it under control. "If you'd told me, maybe things could have been different. Maybe I..."

Smiling, my Father looked at me, and perhaps for the first time in my life, he saw me and asked, "You don't know what it's like to live with someone with mental illness, Charlie? Even in that picture, you have; how many are in that photo? Count them." When he didn't say people in the photos, the hair on the back of my neck stood up.

Looking at the photo, I saw my mother, my father, and my brother. My mother wasn't looking at the camera. I assumed the photo had been taken with a self-timer. I'd seen this same photo in the photo album. When people back then had to get ready for a picture, they scrambled. Thus, my mother not looking directly at the camera wasn't a big deal.

"How many Charlies? How many?" He asked, tearing up. "You assumed it was her rocker in the attic; you assumed that it was her that would sit in the chair and cry and mourn our firstborn. You assumed so many things, and I couldn't tell you, dared not tell you, because the first question you would have asked was...."

"How did he die?" I asked.

Looking at the picture, I followed my Mother's gaze, and I saw Whiro. I looked around wondering where he was, but then remembered he was outside watching for police

How many were in the photo, you wonder, Detective? Well, you've always been smarter than I, why don't you tell me. OK, standing beside my mother with his hand on her shoulder was Whiro, looking so happy, the way he did the day that I framed Johnny for stabbing me, standing as he did, his hand on her shoulder, not that of a family member, Detective, but that of possession. His hand squeezed her shoulder, and the look in her eyes was like my own. It showed the affection we had for Whiro.

"You see him, don't you… she was broken when I found her, Charlie; she had no real family. Father had been a drunk, and he crashed his car into a tree. That was the best thing that ever happened to her. Her mother wasn't much better - alcohol at first, then drugs and rumors of prostitution, and your mother quickly found herself in the foster system.

Life there was not much better. The first person she killed had raped her when she was…," he paused, wiping his eyes, "She killed others. She had this book that she would add names to and scratch them out."

WHERE ARE YOU? I demanded inside my head, but he wouldn't appear, and my father kept talking.

"When you got married, I hoped that the cycle had been broken. I often talked to Kelly before you had kids and some after, but never when you were home. Just catching up, I told her that someday we would talk and that there was plenty of time. I told her that sometimes old wounds are the hardest to heal. She was such a nice woman, and when I mentioned you had an imaginary friend and wondered if the kids did too, she said, "Nope, TV is their friend," and I felt so much joy, hopeful the cycle had been broken.

She often invited me to stay for supper, but I never did. I knew that there was so much I would have to explain. The how you asked about Charlie is that your mother and Whiro killed him."

"What, no, please no!" I shouted, and to my surprise, my father wrapped his arms around me, only looking up long enough to let the funeral director know that it was okay.

With a knowing look, Ross said, "Sure, I won't let anyone in, and your Son may want to exit by the back. I'm seeing a lot of people milling around outside that I don't recognize. I'm sure that they are police. I'm not sure if they're federal, but they're not local cops. Only God takes anyone out of my funeral parlor."

My father gave Ross a nod that said more than just thank you; it was a nod of friendship. He looked back at me and saw the puzzled look on my face. "Ross has been a friend for a very long time. This is a small town, and we take care of our own, Charlie. If you want to come to the house later this week, please do. We can talk more, but I know your next question."

"Why did they kill him?" I was barely able to get the words out through my tears. I wondered where Whiro was. I looked at all the pictures. I could see him in every one of them, but while my mother and I, of course, could see him, my brother and father did not appear to see him. That made me feel good for some reason, Detective.

"She said to keep the blood from raining down. She told me of her imaginary friend, this god only she could see, and to prove it, I would hold up cards, and dammit Charlie, she could name every one of them. She could only do it when he was there behind me. Like a game, Charlie. On the day she killed your brother, I could smell pancakes as I entered the house. All his favorite food was on the table, and somehow I knew.

Raising my fist up to strike her, to kill her, Charlie, to kill her for taking my Son, she held her stomach and said, "This one will be better. You'll see."

You looked so much like your brother. The sadness in my soul was overwhelming, Charlie. I owe you so many apologies. You wonder why I didn't just grab you and run when you were born or when you were a year old. I tried to, but she always knew. I once had you in my arms, and as I opened the car door, she said. "I will kill you where you stand if you take our Son."

He was still holding onto me, Detective. He was still hugging me, and we were both shaking as he continued telling me what I didn't know about myself, "Our Son, Charlie, she wasn't talking about me. She was talking about him. She believed that you were their Son. I don't know if I believe that or whether she passed her mental illness onto you with stories of him when you were in your crib."

Detective, I could not remember ever talking to her about Whiro. I hugged my Father tighter and wished he would stop, but I needed him to continue our story.

"I did talk to the detective and her partner, and still, while I am not sure if Whiro is a god, I believe he exists. I never thought you would get out, but then you got stabbed by Johnny, and you met the Sheriff. It was the first time I had hope. You see, Charlie, I would hear you and her in the room talking with him and listening to his stories. There were a few times I thought it was her voice, but I could not be sure."

No, that is not what happened, Whiro, where are you? I was screaming inside of my head, my father pulled back, "The Sheriff came into your life, the only person that your Mother and Whiro were afraid of. He was such a strong man, striding into the school and slamming that boy against the wall. He took you in, and you finally had the father you deserved."

I was shaking my head, Detective, I never thought my father had ever even noticed me. "Yes,

Charlie, I was at every one of your games. Not up front, but in the back. The Sheriff asked me one day, at the truck stop on Main Street, "Why don't you sit up front?" I told him that you were better off with a role model who could show you the right and just way to get through this world."

"Andy couldn't see him," I whispered. I said it a little louder so my father could hear. "Andy couldn't see him; that is why they killed him. I've been doing research into Whiro, and there is power in generations of these leaches holding onto a family. I bet if we checked further, we'd find out that Mom's father or mother had seen him as well."

Ross opened the door, and motioned for me, pointing toward the back of the room. "You have to go, Son. They're coming up. Go out the back, and take my car. Leave it at the diner. I can walk over there after work."

I looked at my father, wanting to say so much, but holding my hands, he asked, "What will you do now, Son?" For the first time, Detective, I was proud of this man calling me his Son in front of someone.

"I'll come see you in a few weeks or send you a plane ticket where we can talk more. I'm sorry, Daddy, I really am."

"So am I Son, so am I."

I made my way to Ross's car. I didn't hurry. I just walked straight toward it, got in, and then drove out the back entrance. In my rearview mirror, I could see several police officers, both state and local, getting ready. They were going to block off the street and interview everyone who went inside the funeral parlor.

I didn't know that you'd talked to my father. I'm glad now that you did, Detective, and while you may think I'm evil, and I think that you may be right, I will rise again, just like Aphrodite rising from the flames. Now, before you correct me, Detective, I know that Aphrodite didn't actually rise from the flames. She was born from the foam of the sea, but this is a common misconception, so perhaps it's fitting for me.

My journal is on the seat beside me, Detective. 'The Bloody List' looks beautiful on the cover. There's one difference now. I think I recognize the penmanship as that of my mother.

Every question mark has been scratched off, and every person still on my list has been crossed out, and I will no longer pursue them. There is only one name on my list, Detective: 'Whiro, ancient god. Guilty of generational horrors too numerous to name.'

This could be my last letter to you, and if that's the case, I'm sorry because I believe that we've become closer since I first contacted you.

When you talk to my father tell him that I will

reach out someday, I'll have to wait until all the media and police inquiries die down. One thing about society - no matter how important something is in the mass consciousness today, give it a news cycle or two, and the only people who will care are people like you and me.

16

HALLOWED GROUND

WEDNESDAY, AUGUST 29, 2012

How long has it been now, Detective, a year... two? Julie helped my father pack up his home, settle a few affairs, pay his taxes, and sell off the property. A lot of his stuff went to Good Will and the Re-Store place. They seemed to be good charities to donate to. Who is Julie? You remember the guide I told you about. I finally reconnected with her.

Daddy wanted to sell and bring some money, a sort of pride thing. While money is always good, several of the people on my list had money, and some had cash hidden. Getting the combination of a safe from them was never that hard. The Governor had a vault filled with gold coins and a lot of cash. Being a politician pays well, I guess?

I had not seen Whir in a long time and took several precautions with which I hoped to have made myself invisible to him. The first was the hardest thing I've ever had to do since I buried my family, Detective. I went to confession. I'm not Catholic, but I figured it would not hurt to get it all out.

The priest immediately recognized my voice, but perhaps the pain in my voice convinced him to let me finish. I did not know the proper words, so I started the way I'd seen it on television, "Forgive me, Father for I have sinned..."

I told him things I had done and what I had written to you. I told him everything, even some things that will remain between me, him, and God. In the end, instead of telling me to be contrite or whatever it is priests normally do, he asked, "Why?" I noticed he didn't call me 'my son' or anything like that. Who knows, maybe that's only a movie thing.

"You saw him, didn't you?" I asked, and through the screen, I saw him holding his cross tight against his chest.

"I don't know what I saw," he responded.

"I believe you just committed a sin, Father, and

we both know you saw him. Is he a god, a demon, or something else? I don't know what he is, but you saw him, and I bet if you looked at this picture, you would see him behind my mother with his hand on her shoulder."

"No, please," he begged and raised his only arm. The other sleeve was pinned just below where I had cut his arm off. I mumbled something about being sorry that the doctors had failed to re-attach it and put down the picture.

"Sorry, Father, I'm really sorry for what I did to you and for a lot of other things that I have done. I'd blame society or maybe my mother for what she did. But we both know my demon's name, and I need to stop him from doing anything like this in the future; I need your help, please, Father."

The look on his face through the screen said it all. He believed me, and he understood that this was something he had to do. I could tell that if it was in his power, he would help. "Exorcism?" he suggested, not knowing what my plan was.

"No, he doesn't possess anyone. I believe that he's able to, but I think that his spirit if he is a god, could escape."

I didn't tell him that I had talked to other gods and asked them about Whiro. *I don't want to cause this man any more psychic pain.*

I told him something my father had said. "Charlie, you should have seen your mother, how she freaked out when I suggested that you be baptized. I told her that all the babies in my family had been baptized for generations."

I went on to tell him that's what had saved Andy from seeing Whiro.

"Do you believe this?" He asked.

"Yes, I know that he couldn't enter the church grounds, and I know my brother and father couldn't see him, and both were baptized. I can't be baptized, but I need something similar. I need to have a cross. I need to have one that has been blessed by someone like yourself, someone who believes in God and who believes that if I turn myself over to him, he will protect me. I need that father. Can you help me?"

"Of course, follow me." It surprised me how quickly he agreed, but I had no choice but to follow him as he opened the door of the confessional, and both of us stepped out. The church wasn't crowded. We went to his office, where he handed me a cross. It wasn't ornate, but I could feel the power it held. "This was blessed by the bishop, and I use it to pray every night. I prayed for a speedy recovery so that I could get back to my flock and help them."

"You're too good a person, Father. I appreciate this, but I need something more." I explained my plan. He agreed, so I took the cross and gave him the address. Before I left the church, I put the cross over my head and begged for forgiveness.

The address I had given the priest was for a property that I had asked Julie to purchase. She'd placed it in a trust, a small house with a root cellar. Back in the olden days, before refrigeration, some people had cellars, and behind those cellars would be another cellar. That was called root cellar or back cellar.

I had asked my father and Julie to find something like it, and it had worked out perfectly. Some things were just meant to be. My father and Julie sealed everything in the back cellar and put a new door on the front, making sure that there were no cracks. Julie was already baptized, and I hoped that meant that Whiro couldn't see what was in her mind or heart.

The idea was that the church would maintain the property and convert it into storage. Before this conversion, they would seal off the cellar and build on top of it. We would never tell them about the back cellar. Using cinder blocks, we would seal and paint over it.

I didn't know if the priest told the church what was going to be in the old cellar and whether the community would have believed it, but the financial trust we set up was substantial, and they could always use storage. The contract with the church also stated that no one could ever live on the property. I really was trying, Detective. I had no idea whether it would succeed, but as it was, I had a plan. Whiro had told me that gods that still exist are the ones that people believed in. If no one believed in them any longer, they faded away. Before going up to the property, I watched the priest for a while to make sure that he didn't call the police.

Now that I had the cross, I hoped that Whiro wouldn't know what I was up to until it was too late. That night, the priest, Julie, and my father were all waiting down the road in one of the church's vans. Whiro didn't know the location of the property yet, and they tried their best to make sure they weren't followed, and that I did not even know until we got there.

My father told me that the priest had been praying and blessed them both before their journey. He swore that he saw the holy water glowing as the priest splashed it on their foreheads. As they had time, they took part in communion, the first time for my father since he was a kid.

"I asked him to take my confession, Charlie, and after he took mine, he took Julie's." They both hugged after this, tears of sadness and joy on their faces. They both hugged me, and I needed it more than I could ever describe, Detective.

I performed a sacrifice to Whiro in the cellar, and

on my knees, I prayed to him. The doors to the outer and back cellars were open. They had been blessed, but hopefully, he had no way of knowing that; I had my cell phone on, and I had already called Julie. They should have been able to hear everything.

"Whiro, great and powerful Whiro, I am your humble servant, and I need you."

Dagger in my hand, my hand plunged down, but it wasn't an animal or anything living at all that I sacrificed, Detective. I made an even bigger sacrifice.

I plunged the dagger into my Bloody List. His, or my mom's, gift to me. The dagger went straight through it and into a makeshift wooden altar we'd put in the cellar, causing the candles to shake. When it struck, I saw rain, and I saw blood raining down on me, Detective, and I will never forget the immense joy of that moment.

My back was to the door, still on my knees with various idols of Whiro from different incarnations lying on the altar in front of me. I had framed the picture of my mother, Whiro's hand on her shoulder, and put it next to the book.

"You know," was what he said behind me.

"I know, why? Why did you make her kill my brother?"

"He was of no use to me, and I knew that she could give me a replacement."

"Did it hurt? The knife? I wanted to talk to let you know that I am done with you and will never do your bidding again. Whiro" I did not turn, did not look behind me... I wanted, needed him to come around to the front of the altar. Detective, I needed him to be in front of me.

Placing his hand on my shoulder, "Is that why you have a cross in your pocket, Charlie? Do you think you can stop me with that? It doesn't work that way."

I stared down at the picture, the picture of my mother, father, and Andy. He was smiling, Andy was smiling, and I hoped that he hadn't felt any pain. My mother had said to my father that she'd drugged Andy and that he'd been asleep when she'd killed him, but knowing her and knowing Whiro, I wasn't sure whether to believe that.

Whiro saw the picture, moved to the other side, picked it up, and walked deeper into the cellar. I could have jumped up right then, but I needed to give everyone more time. Instead, I pulled the cross out of my pocket and looked at it.

"Did my brother feel pain? No, never mind, I don't need to know that. What I want to know is - if the cross holds no power over the great Whiro, then why not hold it?"

"Is that why you called me here, Charlie? For

games, I've been busy since I left you, and I've found the perfect replacement friend. You should come and meet him. You could be his first. You see, Charlie, I will never let you go; you are mine."

"My father told me everything, said that you visited my mother and told her stories of me. Is that true?"

"Oh yes, Charlie, and she was so proud of you. She had to kill Andy, or there would never have been any blood rain. She loved everything. She laughed at you when I told her how I almost had you kill a priest."

I think I winced then, but with a conspiratorial look, he continued, "Do you have a plan, Charlie? Knife in your shoe, is that it? Some type of specially blessed dagger you want to plunge into my heart. Tell me, Charlie, what are you going to do?"

"You want to know what I am going to do, Whiro? I'll tell you." I stood up and pulled the dagger out of the book and lifted it up, pointed it at him, then turned it, with the tip of the blade resting on my chest.

"I've heard, Whiro, that if someone dies while being possessed by a demon like you, they will take the vile creature with them into hell. Is that true?"

"Demon! DEMON!" he yelled at me, "I am a god, Charlie, I am a god, and you will pay for your insolence. There is nothing you can do to me, nothing at all. I will eat your soul and that of your detective friend and her family. I will leave one alive to continue our legacy until the end of time!"

Whiro threw the picture and frame against the wall. I hoped his yelling would keep him from hearing the others in the outer cellar.

"Well, you know what I'm going to do, oh great and powerful Whiro?" He looked at me, and for all he knew, he did not know this. I smiled, slowly backing out through the doorway. "I'm going to forget you!"

My father slammed the door. I could hear the priest praying as he threw holy water against the door's frame, blessing it, hopefully sealing Whiro inside forever.

We placed a cross on the outside of the door. They either glowed because of the flashlights we carried or because God was protecting us. I will leave that up to you, Detective.

After my father and I had sealed the door, we constructed a new wall to hide all traces of the door. At first, I could hear Whiro screaming inside, and then the priest noticed me shake my head. He took the cross from my hand and, using his only arm, placed it over my neck while he continued praying. The cross he drew on my forehead turned the voice off as if someone had hit the mute button.

It took us all night to finish concealing the door.

DAVID MUSSER

Detective, that night was the first night I didn't see blood raining down when I closed my eyes to go to sleep.

EPILOGUE

MILNER DAILY

Milner Gas Explosion — April 10, 2023 — PRICE $1.25

Milner gas explosion – Seven dead

Monday, April 10, 2023

Sheriff Lois Martenez was looking at her mail, part of it personal and part of it for the office. Several pictures of her family covered the walls and her desk. Kids' drawings also adorned the office walls. Someone looking could track the progression of the child's age based on the type of drawings and various awards.

She smiled as she read the cruise brochure she had printed from a travel site. *What a wonderful trip this will be for us!*

She heard the dispatcher say, "Yes, she's in. I will put you through." Dispatch placed the call on hold, "For you, Sheriff, sounds like a telemarketer."

"Hello, this is Sheriff Martenez. How can I help you?"

"Detective, it's Charlie."

For a moment, the entire world stopped spinning. Lois would have recognized his voice even if she'd never heard it. Charlie, over the years, had sent her different letters and emails to say hello, and while it was true that he saved Shelly, there were a lot of mixed feelings about his disappearance.

Her thoughts returned to what Shelly had said after she'd been freed. "There was only him. I looked the other way when I saw him looking through the hole in the barn. He kept talking about Whiro as if he was real, but Lois, I never saw him."

She remembered interviewing the priest. "Where is the property?"

"Detective, you can subpoena the church, but we own many properties, and unless you plan on digging them all up, you'll never find it."

"So you believe, Father? In Whiro or the god that Charlie always talked about?" Her face was uncharacteristically sarcastic.

"I believe that Charlie believes. I also believe that there is evil in this world. You can't believe in God and the bible without believing in all that goes with it. Did Charlie see a demon or an old god? I don't know."

"Did you see it? Charlie said you saw him."

"No, Detective, I didn't see anything." he'd said while trying not to think about the itching on his missing hand. The doctors had tried to reattach it, but the procedure failed.

She refocused on Charlie. "It's been a while, Charlie. I was sorry to hear about your father. How old was he?"

"My father lived well into his 80s, Detective, I mean, Sheriff, but now is not the time for that. Whiro has escaped. Open your browser and search for Milner Gas Explosion."

The thought of tracking down Charlie using this phone was a fleeting one. Yes, she'd spent many sleepless nights wondering what this monster would send her next, but she knew that Charlie was clever and wouldn't call from his home telephone.

When Charlie heard her gasp, he said, "I knew before I read it in the paper, Detective." He still referred to her with her old position. Lois had since been elected Sheriff. The department was not the same after Shelly retired from active duty. The stress of the incident had been too much for her.

"It says here this happened three days ago; why didn't you call me before?" she demanded.

"I needed to find out if he was free or not," Charlie said apologetically.

"And?"

"Yes, I'm sorry, Detective, he's out, and I know he'll be coming for me, but I also fear that he'll be coming for you."

"Let the bastard come, Charlie; let him bring with him all of the demons from hell, and I promise you, this time, I'll stop him. Let's meet, and we can stop him together!"

Charlie gave her a phone number: "Call me at these times, Detective, and we can plan how to stop him... Have your kids been baptized?"

"We can discuss that in person, Charlie." As soon as she hung up the phone, she called out to her dispatcher, "Nancy, trace that number and this one. Call everyone in." She read out the phone number to her dispatcher. Knowing it would not pan out but needing to try. At least she would be able to call him at specific times, maybe the cell phone companies could track his signal. Charlie had always been a careful man, but maybe he was not as careful as he used to be.

She made a vow to herself. *I will track this son of a bitch down, no matter what it takes.* The fact that he'd saved Shelly never crossed her mind; part of her often wondered if Charlie had set up that situation, and even if not, his activities at the time directed the evil toward Shelly.

Frowning down at the cruise brochure she'd printed, she picked up her cell and called Shelly. The two words she said had been planned since he disappeared. It was two words that Shelly had hoped to never hear from her wife.

Lois remembered how they each promised the other that if these two words were ever uttered, they would pack up and get the children someplace safe. Now that the kids were older and one was about to start college. Lois knew that Shelly would be upset, and she would argue that she should go with them, but she was the Sheriff now, and knew it was her responsibility.

Shelly cringed when she heard, "Whiro's Free."

The End?

FROM THE AUTHOR

"The Bloody List—Letters from a Serial Killer," originally titled "Sex, Blood, and Aftertaste," has been a long time in the making. It's a novel that I stopped and started many times.

The scene about Charlie's family was one of the toughest I've ever had to write, and it almost brought me to tears. Imagining what he was going through and wanting justice for his family was extremely difficult.

I hope that you enjoyed this story. Personally, I hope that Charlie stays locked away in my subconscious. In writing, I'm told there are at least two types of authors: Plotters and Pantsers. The plotters meticulously plan and follow a structured outline before writing the story. The pantsers prefer spontaneity. I feel that I'm something different. You see, I write the stories as they come to me. It's one of those old television shows "Now in Technicolor," the voices in wonderful stereo in my head. Some of what I see is amazingly beautiful, while other scenes are something horrific.

I'm telling you this because if someone were to ask me, "Was Whiro real?" I'm afraid that I would have to be honest and say... "I don't know... and I hope that I never find out."

Find out more about me and an Authors Roundtable that I host at www.dmusser.com.

- David Musser 7/2/2024

To learn more about David Musser and discover more Next Chapter authors, visit our website at www.nextchapter.pub.

MUSIC PLAYLIST

Music helps me focus when writing. I am not sure if it's my dyslexia or what, but I have never been able to focus on one thing at a time, so please enjoy. In case you are curious, I do create the list first before writing.

- To Be A Man – Dax
- Save Me – Jelly Roll
- Halfway to Hell – Jelly Roll
- Wild Thing – Sam Kinison
- Highwayman – The Highwaymen
- (Ghost) Riders in the Sky – Johnny Cash
- Spirit in the Sky – Norman Greenbaum
- One Way or Another – Blondie
- Mississippi Queen – Mountain

MUSIC PLAYLIST

- Stuck in the Middle With You – Stealers Wheel
- Bad Moon Rising – Creedence Clearwater Revival
- Magic Bus – The Who
- Chapel of Love – The Dixie Cups

NEWSPAPER CLIPPINGS

Chapter 1. Milner Daily – The Adonis Killer Strikes Again – Friday April 9, 2010 Price $1.25

Multi-Column Headline: Police Receive Email from alleged serial killer 'Adonis'

Article: The alleged perpetrator sent Detective Martinez the text of the old fable about the scorpion and the frog to explain his motivation. The contents of the email have not been released to the press.

Detective Martinez, has not commented on why she, rather than the investigating officer, received the email. When asked about the alleged serial killer's motivation, she said, "No comment."

Sketch of artit's rendering of Adonis released. The public is asked to keep vigilant...

NEWSPAPER CLIPPINGS

Chapter 2. Milner Daily – The Adonis Killer Strikes Again – Monday April 12, 2010 Price $1.25

Multi-Column Headline: Terrifying Message

Article: Terrifying message from 'Adonis.' "Be afraid. God and vengeance await those who don't follow the path." When asked to comment, detectives had no explanation as to what not following the path entailed. The police ask the public to remain vigilant.

Chapter 4. Milner Daily – Nursing Home Savior? – Monday April 19, 2010 Price $1.25

Article: Nursing Home Savior by Natalie Russell

Several of us are wondering about Adonis, the so-called Serial Killer's motivation and with the latest victim is he a Savior or a Killer?

Detective Martinez's mother was a Shady Pines nursing home resident and a victim of medication theft. M.S. Martinez could not be reached for comment, but an anonymous source told this reporter that a nurse...

Article: Medication Theft on the Rise by Ron Stead

A study by the National Institute of Justice found that 1 in 10 nursing homes had experienced medication theft by staff in the past year.

The average value of the medications stolen was $1,000 per incident.

The theft of medications can have serious consequences for residents including...

Chapter 7. Milner Daily – Reporter's Body Found – Monday May 17, 2010 Price $1.25

Multi-Column Headline: Reporter Latest Victim of Adonis

Article: By Megan Anderson

Kent Green, a reporter for this newspaper, went missing last Friday and has not been seen or heard from since. Kent was a hard critic of the police and was investigating a tip regarding the 'Adonis' serial killer, sent in to the paper's hotline.

Chapter 9. Milner Daily – Drive-Thru Mistake Costs Life – July April 14, 2010 Price $1.25

Multi-Column Headline: Reporter Latest Victim of Adonis

Article: By Megan Anderson

A young man was found dead in his apartment, the latest victim of the alleged 'Adonis' serial killer and what was this man's crime? What did he do that was against the so-called 'way?' I will tell you what he supposedly did. He got an order at the drive-thru wrong, and 'Adonis,' this horrible man that some have called a savior, poured hot melted cheese on this man who had only recently obtained his driver's license.

I've seen the pictures from the crime scene. The blisters and burns he suffered as he tried to claw himself free of the scalding hot cheese, that suffocated him slowly. I will never be able to forget the victim's terrified, hollowed-out eyes.

Chapter 10. Milner Daily – Adonis Kidnaps Priest – Thursday July April 29, 2010 Price $1.25

Multi-Column Headline: Priest Latest Victim of Adonis

Article: By Mark Anderson

Father Halloway of Milner Parish, was kidnapped during his regular evening walk. The prime suspect is alleged serial killer 'Adonis' though it is not clear what Father Halloway might have done to incur the killer's wrath. According to anonymous sources, 'Adonis' has a reason for each one of his killings. The motive in this latest murder remains uncertain.

Chapter 12. Milner Daily – Officer Missing – Wednesday August 18, 2010 Price $1.25

Multi-Column Headline: Detective Martinez's partner missing

Article: By Jeff Pratt

While the police have had the 'Adonis' serial killer listed as their most wanted for some time, the story has taken another bizarre twist. Detective

Martinez's partner Shelly, has been kidnapped and is presumed dead.

An anonymous source inside the police department stated that the alleged killer's communications have turned increasingly frantic. All reserve officers have been asked to report for duty. The police commissioner is forming a new task force to try and recover their missing officer...

Chapter 16. Milner Daily – Where is Adonis? – Wednesday August 29, 2012 Price $1.25

Article: Where is 'Adonis?' by Patrick Madigan

It has been more than two years since serial killer 'Adonis' last contacted Detective Martinez or anyone else at the police department. Some officers believe 'Adonis' had moved on with his kill list, but there are no indications of similar murders anywhere in the country.

"Now that Adonis has been identified, it's only a matter of time. We all know he is laying low," Sherriff Martinez stated...

Article: Local man saves dog from burning building by Brandon Fulco

A local man is being hailed a hero after he rescued a dog from a burning building on Tuesday. The man, who has not been identified, was walking by the building when he noticed smoke pouring from the windows. He entered the building and found a dog chained up in a bedroom. The man was able to unscrew the chain from the wall and free the dog. Both the man and the dog were taken to Milner General Hospital and expect to make complete recoveries.

Asked about the dog, the man said he would try to adopt the...

Article: Community garden party planned for Sunday by L. White

A community garden party, open to everyone, is planned for Sunday on the church lot across from town hall. There'll be food, music, and games.

The party will take place from 12p.m. to 4pm. While food and drinks will be provided, attendees are encouraged to bring some snacks to share.

There will also be a silent auction and a bake sale....

Epilogue. Milner Daily – Milner Gas Explosion – August 10, 2023 Price $1.25

Multi-Column Headline: Milner gas explosion – Seven dead

No article text.

The Bloody List
ISBN: 978-4-82419-894-5
Large Print

Published by
Next Chapter
2-5-6 SANNO
SANNO BRIDGE
143-0023 Ota-Ku, Tokyo
+818035793528

8th October 2024

www.ingramcontent.com/pod-product-compliance
Ingram Content Group UK Ltd.
Pitfield, Milton Keynes, MK11 3LW, UK
UKHW042135171224
452513UK00003B/200